Usborne Stories for Bedtime

Usborne

Stories for Bedtime

Written and retold by Philip Hawthorn

Illustrated by Stephen Cartwright

Designed by Amanda Barlow

Edited by Jenny Tyler

Cover design by Candice Whatmore

Contents

There is a little yellow duck in each story. Can you find it?

Polly and the pixies

Polly was on a very important journey. There wasn't a moment to lose, so she was walking as fast as she could. On her way past a small village green, she noticed the villagers lounging around.

"Why's a little girl like you in such a big rush?" asked a woman.

"I've just been to market to sell a gold ring," said Polly. "My mother is unwell, and we need money to help make her better."

"Well, you'd go a lot quicker with a nice, refreshing drink inside you," said a man. He offered her a full glass. "Here – a present from the village."

Polly was so hot, she took the glass and drank thirstily.

When she'd finished, they produced another, and another, and another. After her fourth glass she said, "Excuse me, where's the toilet?"

An old woman said, "This way my dear. It's all right, you can leave your bag. We'll look after it for you." The other villagers nodded.

When she got back Polly thanked them, picked up her bag and set off. When she was outside the village she looked into her bag, and her stomach turned to jelly. The bag was full of stones.

"I've been robbed!" she wailed, and burst into tears. The sound of tears falling on the ground woke a fairy who was asleep nearby.

"What's the matter?" she asked, yawning. Polly told her how the villagers had stolen her money.

"That village is known to be the meanest in the country. In fact we call the people who live there the Nasties," said the fairy. "This is a job for the pixies!"

She blew into a bluebell flower. In a second they were surrounded by scores of pixies with turned-up noses and pointed ears.

"Who be using the pixie horn?" asked one.

"Me," replied the fairy. "Polly here needs your help."

The pixies murmured worriedly.

"I know you don't like helping humans," continued the fairy. "But if you help Polly you might get a chance to play a trick on the Nasties." At this, the pixies started pulling at their beards with excitement.

"Tell them your story, Polly," encouraged the fairy. Polly took a deep breath and told the pixies exactly what had happened to her.

When she had finished, the pixie chief said, "Me thinks it's time for a pixie fair."

"*A pixie fair! A pixie fair!*" chorused the others.

"What's a pixie fair?" asked Polly.

The chief pixie replied, "Well now, it be a fair held by pixies." They all laughed and pulled each other's beards. "We sets up our stalls, and we sells pixie things like this." Polly watched as he picked up a pine cone and swirled it around very fast. When he opened his hand, the cone had turned into pure gold.

"Here," he said, throwing it to her. "A present from the pixies."

"*A pixie gift! A tricksy gift!*" sang the others, and disappeared.

In the time it took Polly to put the gold pine cone in her pocket, the pixies had reappeared, bringing with them the most beautiful stalls.

"What are you going to sell?" asked Polly.

"*We sell, we sell, whatever we sell!*" the pixies sang, and started to hunt around the clearing. They used their magic to turn pieces of tree bark into chunks of gold, spiders' webs into the finest spun silver, and drops of dew into sparkling diamonds. In no time at all the stalls were groaning with precious things.

Meanwhile, back at the village, the Nasties were counting out Polly's money. When they heard the pixies approaching, they quickly hid it.

"*Come to the fair! Come to the fair!*" chanted the pixies. Then they started to dance around the startled people, singing,

"Flobbity-wee and flibbity-woo,
A pixie fair we have for you,
With gold and silver, diamonds too,
Come to the pixie fair!"

The villagers had heard about little people and how they had secret stores of gold. Sensing the chance to make themselves even richer, they picked up their ill-gotten money and followed the pixies.

When they saw the stalls their eyes goggled with greed. The pixies cleverly charged such bargain prices that the villagers spent all their money.

As the last villager struggled off with her bulging bag of pixie riches, the fairy led Polly out from where they'd been hiding.

"But why did you sell your things so cheaply?" protested Polly. "They don't deserve to have all that after what they did to me." At this the pixies laughed loudly.

"How much would you pay for an old leaf?" said the chief.

"I beg your pardon?" replied Polly.

"*Look! Look! Lookety-look!*" shouted the pixies, pointing at one of the gold leaves that was left on a stall. Polly looked and saw the gold leaf change back into a normal leaf.

"Do you mean all those precious things will turn into ordinary things again?" asked Polly.

"*She's bright, she's bright as a moonlit night!*" sang the pixies.

"And we've got all your money back," said the fairy. "Come on you pixies, hand it over."

The pixies gave Polly most of the money, keeping a little for themselves. (Pixies aren't that nice.) Then they gathered together and sang,
"*Farewell! Farewell! And a fare thee well!*" and with one last chuckle, they were gone.

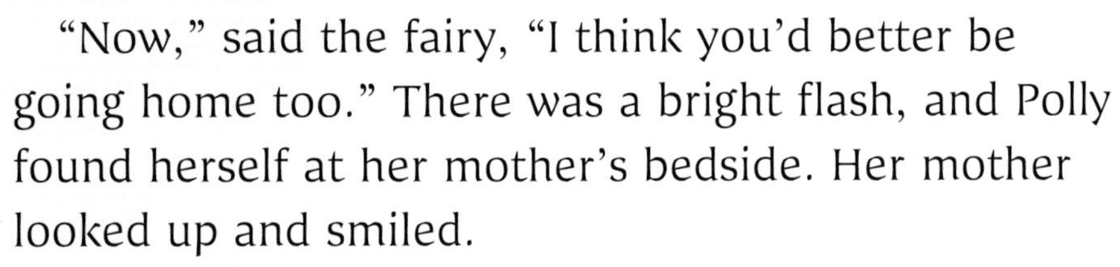

"Now," said the fairy, "I think you'd better be going home too." There was a bright flash, and Polly found herself at her mother's bedside. Her mother looked up and smiled.

"Did you sell the ring?" she asked.

"*I did! I did! I diddly-did!*" sang Polly, smiling back. She reached into her pocket and pulled out the money and the gold pine cone.

The pine cone never turned back, but all the Nasties' things did. If you go to the village today, they'll boast about the time they all bought pixie gold, but they won't show you any of it. And you'll know why, won't you?

Angel

There was once a fairy girl called Angel, who wasn't at all like an angel. She was both proud and spiteful. One day, Angel was out playing hide-and-seek with her friend, Flutterby. This was good fun because they were able to make themselves as small as they liked. Angel was hiding in a daffodil when she heard footsteps. Thinking it was Flutterby, she leapt out, making herself bigger.

"BOO!" she shouted, and laughed. But her laughter soon stopped, for right in front of her was a human boy. Angel disappeared instantly, but she knew she'd been seen.

“Ugh! A human!” she said to herself. “Double ugh! A human boy! I expect he thinks he’s really clever to have seen me, but I’ll show him.”

She spent a few days watching out for the boy, and it wasn’t long before she saw him coming home from school. She followed him to where he lived, then went back to her mother. She had a plan ...

“Mother,” she said, innocently. “If anyone hurt me, would you be angry?”

“Yes,” said her mother.

“Would you punish them?” asked Angel.

“Yes I would, why?” replied her mother.

“Oh, er ... nothing,” said Angel, and she flew off.

That night, the little boy was getting ready for bed when down the chimney flew Angel.

“Hello little boy,” she said.

“Oh, hello,” he said, recognizing Angel at once.

"Do you want to be friends?" asked Angel, smiling a little too sweetly.

"All right," said the boy.

"Good. What's your name?"

The boy was much cleverer than Angel thought, and he was on his guard.

"My name is Me Myself," he said, though it wasn't of course.

"What a stupid name," thought Angel. "What a lovely name," she said. "Let's play chase. Catch me!"

She started flitting around the room. The boy hadn't a chance of catching her as she was so light and quick. But after a minute or two, the naughty fairy fell to the floor, holding her knee.

"Ooohh!" she wailed. "You hurt me, you clumsy human boy."

"I didn't touch you, he said, truthfully.

"Yes you did! Yes you did! Yes you DID!" said Angel. "I'm going to tell. MO-THER!"

Now fairies have amazingly good hearing, and in the flicker of a candle Angel's mother arrived on the roof of the house.

"What's the matter, Angel?" she called down the chimney.

"Someone's hurt my kneeee," she whined. "Are you angry?"

"Yes I am," replied her mother.

"Will you punish them?" she asked.

"Yes. Who did it?" came the reply.

Angel glared at the human boy and smiled vengefully. "The person who hurt my knee was Me Myself," she shouted.

"I see," called her mother. "Well, if it was you yourself, then I will have to punish you yourself."

She waved her magic wand. Before Angel could realize that the boy had outsmarted her, she found herself back in her own bedroom. Angel's mother kept her promise, and her naughty daughter wasn't allowed out for a week. Angel wasn't quite so eager to play tricks after that.

The Hairy Boggart

George Flaxstead was an honest farmer, who just about managed to earn a living. One evening, on his way home, he met the mega-mischievous Hairy Boggart.

"I wants a chit-chat," it said. George Flaxstead knew that boggarts meant trouble and that he'd have to find a way to get rid of it, but he was far too hungry to think now. "Come back in the morning," he said. The boggart left, grumbling.

After George Flaxstead had eaten his supper he thought carefully, and eventually came up with a good plan.

The next day, he found the boggart looking greedily at his field.

"Goodsome land," said the creature. "Grow lovely-jubbly grub for tummy-rumbly boggart."

"There's enough for us both," said George Flaxstead. "We'll go halves on the next harvest, and that's my final offer." The boggart was too lazy to argue, so it agreed.

"Do you want the tops or the bottoms?" said George Flaxstead.

"Umm, topsies," replied the boggart. "Bye-bye, see you at harvest." And it went.

The clever farmer planted a field of potatoes. So when the boggart returned at harvest time, it got the useless leafy tops, and the farmer kept all the lovely plump potatoes which grew underground.

"Next time I want the bottomsies," growled the Hairy Boggart. And it went.

The farmer now planted the field with wheat. So when the boggart again returned at harvest time, it got the useless dry stalks while George Flaxstead got lots of golden grains of wheat.

The boggart was even more angry. " You skillywig!" it said, jumping up and down. "Next year, you grows corn. We cuts corn together and reapers-keepers what we cut."

The boggart was much stronger than George Flaxstead, so it would be able to harvest most of the crop, leaving the poor farmer to starve.

But George soon had another plan.

The next day before the corn harvest, he bought some iron rods from the village blacksmith. After he had painted them golden yellow to match his crop, he stuck them in one end of the field.

The boggart arrived the next day. "Right, ready steady?" it said, sharpening its scythe. "We keeps what we reaps."

"You start over there," said the farmer, pointing to the end with the iron stalks of corn.

The boggart started strongly enough, but then found it tough going. The iron stalks, being so difficult to cut, made it tire very quickly, and they blunted the scythe.

"Getting tired?" taunted George Flaxstead. The Hairy Boggart snarled and gave a huge swipe at the corn. Its scythe snapped, and so did its temper. As it ran off, roaring loudly, George Flaxstead chuckled and shouted after him in his best boggart voice, "Me no scary, hairy fairy." After that, he was never ever bothered by boggarts again.

The endless story

Orlando lived by the sea, and liked to spend time in its company. One evening, he was walking along the beach when he saw a young girl sitting on a rock, combing her hair. As he got closer, he saw that she was a mermaid. Hearing his footsteps, she jumped with surprise.

"You have seen me in the last light of the day," she said. "Now I must grant you a wish. Take this comb and come back at this time tomorrow. Comb the waves and I will come to you. But don't tell anyone you have seen me." Then she slipped silently into the sea and was gone.

That night, Orlando was having a drink with some sailors. As is often the case when men get together, they were boasting by telling amazing stories of the sea.

When it was Orlando's turn he did something very silly. Pulling out the comb he said, "This belongs to a mermaid. Tomorrow I'll have a wish granted." The others laughed scornfully.

"Come and see, if you don't believe me," he said.

So the next evening, Orlando went to the sea's edge. The others crouched behind a fishing boat. Orlando combed the water, and the mermaid rose to meet him. At once the other men rushed forward and grabbed her, shouting things like, "Give us a wish, sweetheart."

Suddenly, they heard a loud roar, and Orlando and the sailors found themselves in Undersea Fairyland. In front of them stood Neptune, king of the sea fairies.

"You have dared to capture a mermaid," said Neptune. "I will release you only if you can tell me a story that never ends."

The sailors each tried to tell the longest tale they could, but no matter how hard they tried to spin out their stories, they eventually dried up.

Finally, it was Orlando's turn. He thought of his walks along the beach, then he began.

"A man decided to polish the beach. He picked up the first grain of sand and polished that, then he picked up the second grain of sand and polished that ..."

Orlando carried on telling how, one at a time, each grain of sand was polished.

When he got to the two hundred and sixty-fifth grain, Neptune said,

"All right, that's enough. I'll let you off this time, but you've been warned." He waved his huge trident and Orlando vanished back to the beach. He never saw the mermaid again, or had his wish.

As for the sailors who had been left behind, Neptune stared at them and said, "You couldn't tell me the story I wanted to hear, so let me tell you one."

He sat down and began to retell Orlando's story about polishing grains of sand. And he went on and on and on and on, far past the part where he'd stopped Orlando.
He went on endlessly.

Orlando's story wasn't all that good, was it? That's because good stories come to an end ...
... like this one.

Sniffer

There were two things that Sniffer always had: a purple silk handkerchief and a cold. That was why he was called Sniffer, because his cold made him sniff all the time.

One Thursday, Sniffer was going to market near Dublin in Ireland. He wanted to buy some vegetables for supper. "I wish I had more money to buy meat for a change. My wife's forgotten what meat tastes like. I'd love to cook some for her," he sighed.

After walking a few more miles, he heard a strange sound from behind a hedge. He peeped through it and saw a small man sitting on the ground, mending a shoe. Sniffer looked at the man and suddenly realized that he was a leprechaun.

Sniffer immediately remembered his grandmother's advice. "If you ever see a leprechaun, catch hold of him," she had said. "Don't let go, and don't take your eyes off him for a second, or he'll be off with a laugh and a tickle. Ask him where his pot of gold is buried, and he'll have to tell you."

So Sniffer waited until the leprechaun reached into his bag for another nail, then he made his move.

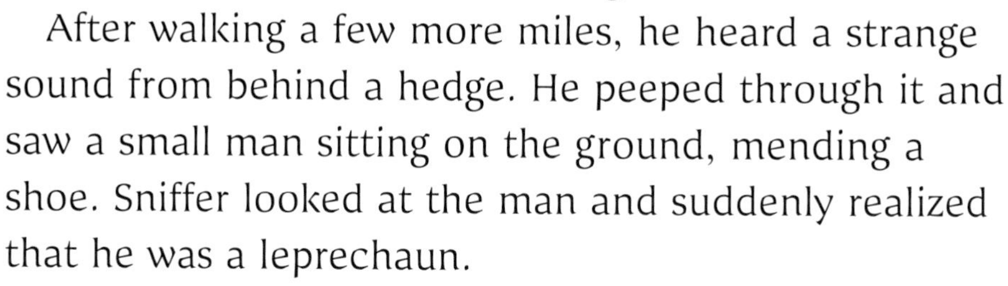

"Gotcha!" he called, as his hand tightened around the leprechaun's arm. He was surprised that the leprechaun just laughed.

"Ah! That's caught me well and good, so it has," he giggled. "To be sure, you've got the better of me."

"Yes," replied Sniffer, a little uneasily. "Now I want your pot of gold."

"Well, if you just let go of my arm, I'll lead you to it." Sniffer started to loosen his grip, then remembered his grandmother's warning not to let go. "I know what you're up to," he said, and he held on even more tightly.

"Well now, if you aren't the smartest lad in Ireland," said the leprechaun. "I reckon you're so smart you'd always help a beautiful girl in trouble."

"Of course I would," said Sniffer.

"Well, there's one behind you who's being chased by a ferocious bull," said the little man, pointing over Sniffer's shoulder.

Sniffer was about to turn around when he again remembered the advice his grandmother had given him not to look away.

"You little pickle," said Sniffer, staring at the leprechaun even harder. "Now, it's gold time!"

The leprechaun started out across the field, trying without success to wriggle himself free. By now, Sniffer was sniffing quite a bit because he hadn't been able to blow his nose while holding onto the leprechaun. Eventually, they arrived in the middle of a huge field of beautiful poppies.

"It's under this poppy," said the leprechaun, pointing to one. "Dig down deep and you'll find the gold."

"I just need to go and get a spade," said Sniffer. "How will I know which is the right flower when I get back?"

"I'll wait here and tell you," the leprechaun replied, his eyes growing brighter.

"I'm not falling for that," said Sniffer. At this point, he decided to blow his nose. He reached into his pocket and pulled out the purple silk handkerchief. Then a thought came to him.

"Tie this handkerchief to the poppy," Sniffer said. The leprechaun did as he was told.

"Promise me that you won't take it off. Cross your heart and hope to die, or whatever leprechauns say."

"I promise," said the leprechaun.

"Right," said Sniffer. Then he let go of the leprechaun and ran off to his house.

When he got back to the field, he saw that the leprechaun had not removed the silk handkerchief. What he had done was tie identical handkerchiefs to all the other poppies in the field. It would take years to dig under all of them.

"Oh cabbage," said Sniffer. But at least he now had hundreds of silk handkerchiefs. He gathered them all together and put them in the bag he'd brought for the gold.

He then went to the market, where simply by selling three of the silk handkerchiefs he was able to earn enough money to buy a nice piece of meat and some vegetables, which he cooked for his wife that night. And he still had hundreds of silk handkerchiefs left – which was not to be sniffed at.

Brave words indeed

Charlie Chumpchop, the shepherd, had left his flock in the care of a friend and gone off for a good walk. As he walked along, he saw a small flute on the ground. He picked it up. It was silver, and so fine that it weighed hardly anything. He put it to his lips and blew. There came the sweetest, purest note you could imagine, and a tiny fairy appeared.

"Can I have my flute back please?" she said. Charlie handed it over.

"Ha! You could have asked for anything," said the fairy. "Don't you know I am bound to reward you? But since you are an honest boy, I will give you something." She reached into her pocket and gave Charlie three small, round, white things. "These are magimints. When you eat one, it will give you exactly the right words to say."

Then she put the flute to her lips and disappeared, leaving the trace of a fairy tune in the still morning air.

Charlie put the magimints into his pocket and headed for the city. At the palace there was a lot of activity.

"I suppose they're having a royal lunch," he thought, looking at the array of noblemen arriving on dashing horses. He went closer and found himself outside a room in which the important guests were talking excitedly.

"You're just in time, sir," said a guard, ushering Charlie into the room and closing the door behind him. The conversation stopped, and twenty pairs of eyes stared at Charlie; stares that would pierce steel.

"What do you want?" said a tall knight in gold tights.

"I... I..." stammered Charlie.

"The poster does say *anyone* can try for the princess' hand," said a fat lord in a fur-trimmed coat, indicating the poster on the door. As conversation began again, Charlie read the poster. This is what it said:

HIS ROYAL MAJESTY KING ROLLMOP III
SEEKS A HUSBAND FOR HIS DAUGHTER,
HER ROYAL HIGHNESS PRINCESS SALAMI.
A TEST WILL BE SET ON THURSDAY NEXT.
ANYONE IS WELCOME.

"That seems a bit unfair on the princess," thought Charlie. "Oh well, I bet I'm as strong and fast as any of this bunch." Then he saw some small writing at the bottom

UNSUCCESSFUL CANDIDATES WILL BE EXECUTED.

"Executed!" yelled Charlie.

"Oh, don't worry," said a kindly baron. "We all have armies, the king wouldn't dare harm us."

"But the only army I've got is an army of sheep," thought Charlie in dismay. Before he could think of escape, the trumpeter next to him blew a fanfare which made Charlie jump. Some big doors opened, and in came the king and princess. They sat down on their thrones.

The king had a small moustache that twitched nervously. The princess looked incredibly sulky. She was the sort of person who never showed enthusiasm for anything.

"My lords," said the king. "I have decided that the princess shall marry whoever can say the bravest words. Is that all right, my dear?" He looked at Princess Salami.

"Don't care," she said, without the slightest interest.

"And, of course, the rest of you will die," continued the king. "Who's first?"

A rather thin man called Baron Waste stepped up. "I could slay a fierce dragon with my trusty sword."

The next, Sir Dean Tynne, said, "I could slay two fierce dragons with my knife." Each of those that followed tried to outdo those before him. Then Count Üptaten said, "I could slay a hundred huge, hungry dragons armed only with a small twig and a paper cup."

The king glanced at his yawning daughter. There were only two people left.

The first, Sir Pryze, stepped forward. He was tall, handsome and very rich. "My words of bravery are not human. For what could be braver than the words of the king of the beasts, the lion. Grrrrrrrrrr!" And he growled fiercely. During the applause, the princess yawned again.

"You boy," said the king, pointing at Charlie. "You're last."

Charlie walked up to the throne. His face was frozen in panic, his throat was dry and his knees were like jelly.

Suddenly, he remembered the magimints the fairy had given him. He put one into his mouth.

"Your Majesty," he began. All at once, it felt as if his tongue had a mind of its own. "Did you hear about the dragon who was in a film? She became very flame-ous."

There was a shocked silence. "Oh dear, maybe that magimint had gone stale," thought Charlie, popping another one into his mouth. Immediately, he said, "Did you hear about the lord who was chased by a lion? He was Lord Claude Bottom."

"How dare you!" bellowed the king. He was just about to order Charlie's immediate execution when he heard a sound that made him stop. The princess was laughing, so hard that tears were pouring down her cheeks. The king had never seen her laugh before.

"You have always tried to impress me," she said, giggling. "At last someone has made me happy."

"Come to think of it, telling jokes was incredibly brave ... you win, my boy," the king said.

So Charlie and the princess were married, and lived happily for many years.

The bath assault

Wexon-by-Glade was a pretty country town. It was well-known for its neat streets and tidy parks, and as the home of Blubberbelly Bath Salts. Mr. Blubberbelly was fat and rude, unpopular and selfish, and his heart was as hard as cement; but he did make the best bath salts in the country. "Only sensational smells," he'd boast.

The River Glade, which ran behind Mr. Blubberbelly's factory, did not smell very nice, however. It had a strange green tinge, with bubbles floating on the top. The fish were often ill, and so were the river sprites who looked after it. In the end two of them went to see Oberon, king of the fairies.

"It's not fair," said Pondweed. "We try to look after the river and everything that lives in, on or by it."

"The situation is very, very bad," said Ripple.

"I know," said Oberon. "I think we should go and have a look around Mr. Blubberbelly's factory."

"But he only makes sensational smells," said Ripple. "It says so on the front."

"We'll see," said the king.

They made themselves invisible, flew into the factory, and came to a noisy room with a large boiling tub and lots of pipes and tubes.

There was a wonderful smell of lemon in the room.

"This is the room where they make the bath salts," said Oberon. Then he led them through a door marked 'Waste Room'. The smell was terrible.

"Yukkity ugh!" said the sprites once inside.

"You see, whatever you make, there's always waste," began Oberon, "It's like with cooking. You can make the tastiest food, but there's always something such as carrot tops, onion skins or egg shells, to get rid of. Let's see what Mr. Blubberbelly does with the waste from his factory, shall we?"

They found a pipe which ran out of the room and followed it. It wound around lots of corners and eventually went outside. From the end, thick gunk was pouring straight into the river.

"Stinky-poo!" said Pondweed.

"It's time to have a word with Mr. Blubbersmelly," said Oberon. So that night, the three fairies visited the factory owner in his house. "How dare you come in here!" he shouted. "I'm just about to have my bath. I want to try out my new lemon bath salts. Buzz off." (Mr. Blubberbelly looked soft, but his heart was as hard as cement.)

Now it doesn't do to shout at a fairy, especially if he's a king. Oberon waved a magic spell over the new bath salts and led the fairies away.

"What was the spell, your Majesty?" asked Ripple.

"Wait until tomorrow," came the reply.

Early the next morning, the fairies flew to the market square, and what they saw there made them gasp. Mr. Blubberbelly was sitting in a bath of cement.

"I changed the bath salts to cement powder," said Oberon. "When he mixed it with water and sat in it, it set. Then just for good measure, I made it move over here." They flew down and perched on the edge of the bathtub.

"You did this to me!" fumed Mr. Blubberbelly. "I can't move!"

"You expect nice clean water in your bath," said Oberon. "The river creatures expect the same in their river. Only you can help them."

"Never!" said the arrogant man. "I'm not going to be ordered around by a bunch of fairies."

"Suit yourself," said Oberon as they flew away. "You'll only be free when you've found a way to say you're sorry."

Mr. Blubberbelly folded his arms. "I shall not be moved," he shouted.

"You're right there," said a woman on her way to work. "It'd take an elephant to move that bathtub." Then she called to the others, "Look at old Blubberguts!" Soon, there was a crowd of people looking and laughing at him.

This went on all morning. At lunchtime he started to feel hungry. In the afternoon, he was hungry, cold and bursting to use the toilet.

"All right," he yelled as night fell. "I give in! You win!" But there was no one around. "I know how awful the river is! I will change things, I promise!" But all that could be heard was the wind whistling around the town hall tower.

In the end, he started to cry. As the tears fell onto the cement, they melted it. He climbed out of the sludgy bath and walked home. The next day, he arranged for trucks to take away all the factory waste.

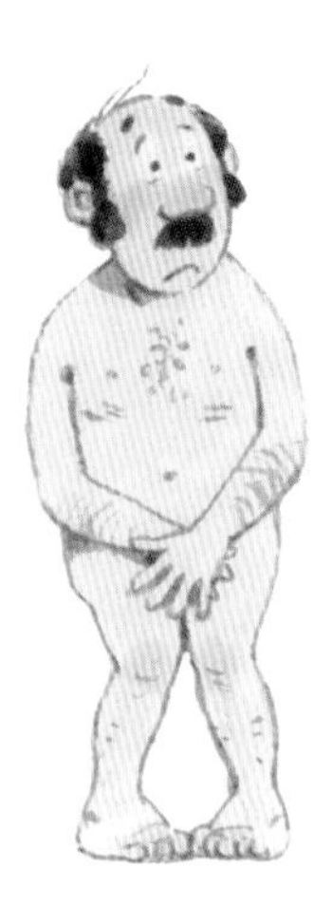

Mr. Blubberbelly's heart remained generous and kind. It had been hard as cement, but now it was melted.

The tooth fairy

Alice liked collecting things. Unfortunately they were things that made her parents say, "Oh please! Really, Alice!" For example, she had the two stitches from when she'd cut her chin, a dead beetle she'd found in the bathtub, and lots more. She kept everything in matchboxes, wrapped in tissue paper. Her father called them her horror boxes.

When a tooth fell out, however, there was no way she'd keep it: teeth were for the tooth fairy.

One evening, Alice sat in her room wiggling a loose tooth with her tongue and wrapped her Aunt Megan's birthday present (a bar of strawberry soap). Aunt Megan always spent her birthday with Alice's family. Aunt Megan was fat and loud, wore lots of make-up and gave the most disgusting kisses. She hated the horror boxes even more than Alice's parents.

The doorbell rang and Alice's mother shouted up the stairs, "Al-ice! Come and say hello to your aunt!"

Alice flumped down the stairs. Excited grown-up babblings were already in full swing, and as she appeared Aunt Megan gushed,

"And here's dear Alice. Haven't you grown!"

Alice winced and thought, "Of course. That's what children do."

"Come and give your auntie a kiss," said Aunt Megan. Alice saw the big, pink lips coming towards her, and then ... Slurpy-Slobber! Perfume-Smelly! Sticky-Wet kiss. Eeyuurrgh!

The force of the kiss made not one, but both of Alice's front teeth come out. She used her tongue to explore the new warm holes in her gums. Then she spat the teeth into her hand and held them under her aunt's nose.

"Aunt Megan, look what your kith did!" she lisped. Aunt Megan did look, and turned pale.

"Oh my goodness!" she wailed. "How re-volt-ing!" Then, with a sweep of her hand she sent the teeth flying to the floor. While the grown-ups went to recover with cups of tea, Alice picked up the teeth and went to her room.

She was furiously thinking. "How dare Aunt Megan treat my teeth like that," when she had an idea. She put one tooth under her pillow. Then she unwrapped the soap, put the bloodiest tooth in a matchbox, and wrapped it up. "Happy Birthday, Aunt Dragon," she said. And climbed into bed.

Alice woke in the night feeling even more fed up, and decided to put the other tooth in Aunt Megan's present too. She reached under her pillow and, to her great surprise, grabbed a tiny hand. As she brought it out, a silver glow appeared. It was a fairy, carrying Alice's tooth and a sack.

"You're the tooth fairy," said Alice. "How you glow."

"Of course. That's what fairies do," said the fairy. Pointing at the tooth she said, "Nice one."

"What happenth to the teeth you take?" lisped the front-toothless Alice.

"I'll show you," said the fairy. She took Alice's hand and they both flew out of the window.

To start with, they visited the bedrooms of sleeping children. The fairy disappeared under each pillow with a silver coin and emerged with a tooth, which she put in her sack. Then they flew to the North Pole, to collect a baby polar bear's tooth from under it's pillow of snow. And finally, to a smoky-hot mountain for a huge dragon's tooth which lay under a pillow of hot coals.

"What do you do with the teeth?" said Alice.

"Come on, I'll show you," said the fairy.

They flew for ages, then the fairy started to dive. They were heading for the middle of a ring of mushrooms in a field. Nearer and nearer, faster and faster they got, until Alice was so scared she closed her eyes.

"Hold on tight!" called the fairy.

Scrunch! Whizz! Fizz! Whooooosh!

Alice opened her eyes. The moon seemed enormous, and the stars winked and twinkled brightly. The trees glowed in the moonlight and the rivers looked like liquid silver.

"Welcome to Fairyland," replied the tooth fairy.

The air was as fresh as mountain air, but warm as a summer's evening. As they flew, Alice felt as if she would always be this happy. They soon came to a brightly lit house and looked through a window at the frantic activity inside.

"What'th going on?" said Alice.

"Well, I'm not the tooth fairy, I'm a tooth fairy. There are lots of us. Come on," said the fairy, and they went inside. "We wash all the teeth in here," she said, pointing to a huge bath. They went into the next room. "This is where the most important thing happens. Watch."

The clean teeth were put into a pot and the lid closed. The fairies gathered around. They pointed their fingers at the pot and sang a fairy song. Soon, the air shimmered with magic. Alice had never seen anything so totally exciting. When the pot was uncovered, it was full of dazzling, shiny pearls.

"We're the only fairies with this magic," said the tooth fairy, proudly. "In this pot were the teeth of rich children and poor children, good children and naughty children. Yet each one has made a perfect pearl. Out of the ordinary comes the amazing!"

Alice had breakfast with the tooth fairies, then it was time to go. She waved goodbye, and as they flew back, tired from her busy night, Alice dropped off to sleep.

Alice woke in her own bed. She mistily remembered what had happened. Had she dreamed it all?

"Come on, Alice!" came a yell from downstairs. "Aunt Megan is waiting for her present."

Alice looked at the clock: half past nine! She leapt out of bed, grabbed her aunt's present, dashed downstairs and handed it over. As Aunt Megan was opening it, Alice remembered the tooth inside. She turned red and tried to think of an excuse to leave, but it was too late.

Aunt Megan opened the matchbox.

"Alice!" she said, her eyes widening. "How absolutely ... wonderful." She took from the box a pair of beautiful pearl earrings. "Put them on me, dear."

Alice did. When she looked at her aunt afterwards she thought, for the first time, that she wasn't so bad after all. "Out of the ordinary cometh the amathing," she lisped.

"Beg your pardon, dear?" said Aunt Megan.

"Oh, er, nothing," replied Alice. "Breakfatht anyone?"

The Silly-Willies

King Dominic lived all alone in a huge castle in a town, the name of which no one could ever remember. This particular day, his old friend Whizz the magician was visiting.

"It's the strangest thing," said the king after dinner. "My loyal subjects have been extraordinarily silly lately. Yet whenever anyone says they're silly, they get very upset. They're a right bunch of silly-billies."

"It sounds more like the Silly-Willies," said the magician. "Silly-Willies are naughty fairies who roam around, staying in different towns. They creep into bedrooms at night and whisper silly things to do into someone's ear. That person is then in a Silly-Willy spell. Leave it to me, tomorrow I'll get to the bottom of it."

The next day, Whizz put on his best magician's robe and sauntered into town. On his way he walked over a hill. On top, standing under a tree, were two very frightened men.

"What's the matter?" asked Whizz.

"We're worried," said one, quivering.

"See that apple," said the other, pointing to the only apple in the tree.

"Yes," said Whizz.

"Well, what if there was a dreadful snow storm?" said the man.

"... With a strong wind," said the second.

"... The apple would blow off the tree ..." said the first.

"... And roll down the hill ..." continued the second.

"... And as it rolled it would make a huge snowball ..."

"... And what if a small girl was standing in its way ..."

"... Wearing a thick balaclava so she couldn't hear anything ..."

"... And it squashed her," concluded the second. They looked at each other and burst into tears.

"It would be so terrible," they sobbed together.

"Yes," said Whizz. "But what if it didn't snow? After all, it is the middle of August. And anyway," he said, picking the apple and biting it. "What apple?" At this, they turned to him and said, "What do you know?" Then they walked off.

Whizz carried on. "That's definitely one case of the Silly-Willies," he muttered to himself. Suddenly, from inside a house he heard:

Thump-thump-thump-thump ... Crash! Ow!

Whizz knocked and went inside. In the bedroom upstairs was a man who had hung his trousers on a chest of drawers. He was trying to put them on by running up and jumping into them, but each time he crashed into the drawers, banging his knees painfully.

"Why don't you step into them and pull them up with your hands?" said Whizz.

"What do you know?" said the man, rudely. "You don't even wear trousers. Now if you'll excuse me ..." As Whizz left he heard:

Thump-thump-thump-thump ... Crash! Ow!

That was another case of the Silly-Willies – and he found lots more that day.

As Whizz was returning that night, he saw some people standing around the town pond, murmuring.

"What's the matter?" said Whizz.

"The moon's fallen into the pond," said a woman, pointing into the pond at a reflection of the moon.

"That's only its reflection," said Whizz.

"What do you know, smarty-pants?" she said.

"I'll show you," he replied. He took a stick and stirred up the surface of the water, shattering the reflection into a million rippling fragments.

"He's broken the moon!" shouted a man.

"Get him!" said another.

They chased Whizz all the way back to the castle.

That night, he told King Dominic all about his findings.

"What *can* we do?" said the king.

"Well," began Whizz. "The Silly-Willies get into people's bedrooms through keyholes. If everyone blocks them up, they'll move on somewhere else. As they aren't in the castle, you needn't bother."

The king issued a proclamation, and everyone blocked their bedroom keyhole. The next day, there were no cases of the Silly-Willies anywhere in the town. That night, Whizz was ready to move on.

"I can't thank you enough," said the king. Then as Whizz trotted off on his horse he added, "But where are the Silly-Willies now?"

"Who knows?" replied the magician. "The Silly-Willies come and go like the wind. They could be anywhere, absolutely anywhere. Thanks for having me. Goodbye."

The king watched his friend disappearing and then saw the drawbridge being raised. Suddenly, he stared with horror into the moat.

"Whizz!" he shouted with all his might. "Whizz! Come back! It's the moon! It's fallen into the moat!"

The magician's assistant

Alex was a magician's assistant, although he hadn't learned any magic, yet. He assisted a magician named Madge, a good woman whose main goal was to find spells to cure people's ills and help them in various ways.

Madge's spell room was amazing. The walls were lined with all sorts of bottles and jars containing the strangest things you could imagine, and many you couldn't. There were also books, funny-shaped equipment, spiders' webs, dust, and the sort of grimy things that you find in places that haven't been properly cleaned for years.

One morning, Madge looked particularly excited. "It's time for magic," she said. "I need the Magispells book."

"I'll get it for you," chipped in Alex.

"Alex, you know I have told you never to go near my Magispells book. Magic is a serious business. I work only for good, but there is also evil magic. Often the two are not that far apart."

Alex sulked. "When am I going to do some magic?" he grumbled. Madge ignored him and opened the enormous book. "Are you ready, Alexander?"

Alex nodded and stood up lazily.

"I'm doing a specially whizzzy spell today – and that's 'whizzzy' with three 'Zs'. Now, let's see, I need some powdered chestnut, three tears of laughter and that caterpillar skin I asked you to drench in the beams of a full moon." Alex collected them and gave them to Madge.

"Thank you," she said, mixing them together.

"All I need now is some fluff from the pouch of a kangaroo." Alex went to the cupboard and looked at the jar.

"It's empty," he called.

"Oh tinkle," said Madge. "That means I'll have to go and borrow some from my friend Cuppen Sorcerer. I won't be long. Would you make a start on the clearing up please, but don't touch my spell. Toodle pipple." And she left. Alex looked at the mess and sighed.

"It's going to take me ages," he said to himself. Just then Catsby, Madge's cat, gave a loud meow.

"You're right, Catsby," said Alex. "What a bore." Catsby purred and jumped onto the Magispells book. As Alex picked her up, he had an idea. There must be a tidying spell in the Magispells book. After all, he told himself, it would help Madge.

Alex opened the book and leafed through the pages. "Let's see, 'Cure For Hiccups' ... no, 'Spell To Turn Mud Into Chocolate' ... hmm, nice but not for now ... here we are: 'Tidying Up Spell'."

It looked quite easy really. He gathered the ingredients and mixed them together. Then came the magic words.

"Ibblibum bottium, fattus wobblium ..." he chanted. But Madge's handwriting was so hard to read that he started to make mistakes, "*Er ... capsicum sillius billium ...* is that *fillius dillium*?"

He was just about to give up when there was a huge thunderclap. Green smoke emerged from the book, wound itself in spirals and became a tall, green man with large, hairy ears. Alex was rooted to the spot.

"O most gracious master," said the creature, bowing. "I am your loyal servant, Hairylugs. Your wish is my command. You have but to ask. I am all ears."

"Mmm," Alex thought, "Your ears are pretty big." Then he said, "Great! Would you do a bit of tidying up for me, please?"

"No sooner said than done," said Hairylugs.

Alex had never seen anyone work so quickly. Hairylugs was like a green whirlwind. Jars flew back into place and bottles rattled onto their shelves. Alex smiled. "That'll show Madge," he thought. "Now she'll have to let me do more magic."

Then things started to go a bit wrong. The creature started to tidy Madge's bench.

"No, leave that," said Alex. "That's enough." But Hairylugs just ignored him and carried on. Madge's new spell was swept into the waste bin. Then all the cobwebs and dust were brushed away, until the room was shining. Finally he picked up Catsby and put her away in a cupboard.

"What now, O master?" said Hairylugs.

"Er, nothing. You can go, thanks," replied Alex.

"What NEXT?" boomed Hairylugs.

Alex began to feel a bit scared, and well he might.

Because instead of calling a helpful fairy, he had called a mischievous goblin, who was now yelling, "I want an ORDER!"

Alex said the first job that come into his head, "Water the plants."

"No sooner said than done," said Hairylugs, but with a sneer rather than a smile. He went into the garden and poured gallons over each plant, so that the garden was awash. Then he came inside and started to water the house plants. He used a huge bucket, which he kept on filling and emptying over the pots with a great Sploosh!

"Stop! Stop!" said Alex, as the water started to rise over his ankles.

"Why?" bellowed Hairylugs. Sploosh! "I have to obey your command, you worm!" Sploosh! The water kept rising, and Alex began to cry.

"Ha! Ha!" laughed the goblin. "Trying to help me water with your tears?" Sploosh!

Suddenly, the door burst open and Splo-WOOSH! Madge was knocked over by a tidal wave.

She took one look at Alex's face and Hairylugs' frantic activity and instantly summoned up all her wisdom and fairy knowledge. She took out her wand and challenged Hairylugs to a battle of magic.

There were massive explosions as spells fizzed and crackled all around. Alex crouched behind the bench, wide-eyed as Madge and Hairylugs changed each other into all sorts of amazing things.

Then Madge came across the waste bin containing her spell. She took the kangaroo fluff from her pocket and mixed it in.

She yelled the spell at Hairylugs, who instantly screamed, became a cloud of green smoke and disappeared up the chimney.

"Whew!" said Madge. "It was a good thing I was working on a spell to get rid of goblins."

Alex thought he was going to get the biggest scolding of his life, but Madge decided he'd learned his lesson well enough. All she said was, "You see, not much separates good magic from evil magic; it can be as little as a badly made spell."

At this point, they both heard a scratching noise.

"Hairylugs!" screamed Alex, diving under a chair. Madge went over to a cupboard and opened it. Out skipped Catsby, who stretched, yawned and went to her bowl to remind everyone that it was time for dinner.

The fairy at the well

Once there was a man who lived with his two sons. The elder, Oscar, was the spitting image of his father. This meant he was good-looking, grumpy and greedy.

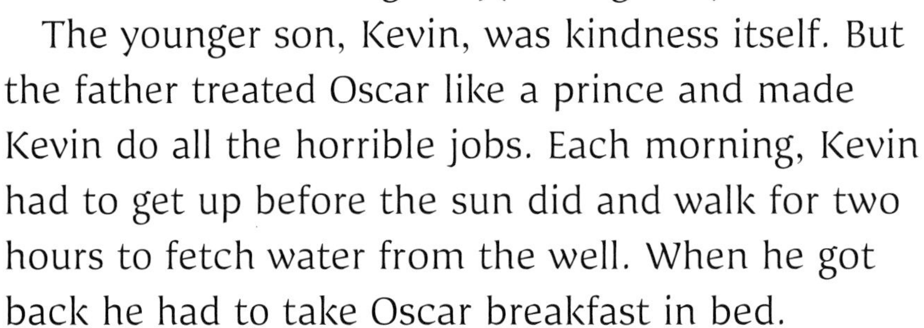

The younger son, Kevin, was kindness itself. But the father treated Oscar like a prince and made Kevin do all the horrible jobs. Each morning, Kevin had to get up before the sun did and walk for two hours to fetch water from the well. When he got back he had to take Oscar breakfast in bed.

One day, while he was at the well, Kevin was approached by a scruffy, old woman.

"May I have a drink, please?" asked the woman.

"Certainly," said Kevin. He pulled up the bucket of water and poured some into a jug for her.

The woman was really a fairy who had made herself poor to see just how kind Kevin was. She said, "From now on, with every word you say, a flower or precious stone will fall from your mouth."

When Kevin got home his father barked, "You're five minutes late."

"Yes, I'm sorry Dad," said Kevin. A diamond, two tulips and a ruby fell onto the kitchen floor.

"A-ma-zing!" said his father. Then he made Kevin tell him what had happened, which made more jewels and flowers come out of his son's mouth. When Kevin had finished, his father sent him to clean out the pigsty while he picked the jewels out of the wonderful pile on the floor. Then he called Oscar.

"There's an old woman down at the well," he said, his eyes burning with greed. "Give her some water and she'll give you something amazing."

"Do it yourself," said the incredibly rude son.

"Go, or you'll feel my shoe on your bottom," shouted his father. Oscar picked up the jug and stomped off.

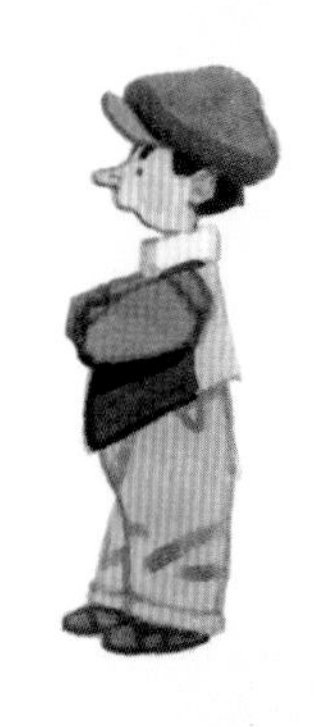

By the time he reached the well he was hot and sweaty. He had just sat down when a young woman came up to him.

"Hello, sir," she said. "Would you kindly get me some water, please."

Oscar looked up. "Oh, Miss La-di-da wants some water, does she?" he said with a sneer. "Get it yourself."

The girl was the same fairy as before, only this time she wanted to see just how rude Oscar was.

"Every word you speak shall turn into something horrible," said the fairy, and disappeared.

Oscar walked home without the jug. When he arrived his father said, "Did you meet her?"

"No, I didn't," puffed Oscar. Two rotten eggs and a dead beetle fell from his mouth.

"Ugh!" yelled the father. "This is Kevin's fault."

Then he ran off to slap his younger son. However, Kevin heard him coming and left the house. He went to a big city, where his wealth could help the poor.

As for Oscar, he now had to do all the jobs around the house. He moaned so much that the house was soon filled with nasty things, so his father threw him out. The fairy went back to Queen Mab, the queen of the fairies, and sang her this song,

"A person speaking gentle words,
Spreads joy as great as jewels.
But nasty mouths are worth as much
As kindness is to fools."

The disobedient dog

"Alfie, will you come here!" yelled Mr. Truffle at his disobedient dog. But Alfie just sat in the middle of the park and looked around at the beautiful summer's day.

Mr. Truffle walked on until he arrived at the gate, then he turned and shouted, "Alfie, come HERE!" Alfie sniffed the air, made a lazy snap at a passing bumble bee, then lay down on the grass. All the other people in the park looked and smiled, just as they did every day. It was quite entertaining to see Mr. Truffle getting angrier and angrier.

"Well, blow me down!" said Mr. Truffle, turning red. "Everyone else's dog obeys them, why can't mine?" He walked out of the gate in the direction of his house. When a minute had passed, Alfie got up and trotted happily after him.

Once more he'd shown everyone who was the boss.

"That dog! That dog!" puffed Mr. Truffle when he got home. He was just about to close the door, when Alfie walked in, sat down and started a long, slow scratch.

"And you can stop that!" shouted Mr. Truffle. But Alfie didn't, of course. He kept on showering the kitchen with hairs, bits of twig and grass.

"Well, blow me down!" said Mr. Truffle.

The following day, Mr. Truffle walked Alfie in the forest next to the park. He threw a stick, but Alfie just trotted off in the other direction, with a look which said, "Fetch it yourself." Suddenly, there was a bright flash and in front of Mr. Truffle appeared a small dog. It had a shiny gold collar and hovered above the ground using tiny silver wings.

"Hello," it said. "I'm your furry dogmother."

"Well, blow me down!" said Mr. Truffle.

"I'm from the land of pixie poodles, leprechaun labradors and spritely spaniels. Name a wish and it shall be done."

"I wish that Alfie would obey me," said Mr. Truffle, after no more than a second's thought.

"All right," said the fairy dog. It wagged its tail, causing a spray of shimmering stars to fall on Mr. Truffle. "He will now obey every single word you say." Then it was gone.

Mr. Truffle rubbed his eyes. "Well, blow me down!" he said again. "It must have been a dream."

He walked out of the forest into the park. "Come on Alfie," he said without thinking. The next thing he knew, there was a rumble of approaching paws as Alfie came rushing up and walked obediently at his master's side. Mr. Truffle stopped in amazement.

"Are you feeling all right, Alfie?" he asked. Alfie stared at him, panting eagerly, looking as though he was waiting for a command. Mr. Truffle hardly dared say anything.

"Sit," he said at last. Alfie obeyed. "Lie down." Alfie obeyed. "Roll over." Again, Alfie obeyed. Mr. Truffle picked up a stick and threw it into the middle of the park. By now, people were starting to watch.

"Alfie ..." said Mr. Truffle. Alfie sat up, alert. "Alfie, fetch!" Alfie set off like a streak of lightning, and grabbed the stick with his mouth as he slid past. Then, his feet scampering wildly, he tore back to Mr. Truffle, dropped the stick at his feet, and sat waiting for his next order.

The people in the park could not believe it. Mr. Truffle could not believe it. He just scratched his head and said,

"Well, blow me down!"

But unfortunately, the magic was still working. Alfie obeyed – and blew him down!

Fairy Nuff

Fairy Nuff wasn't beautiful and graceful like other fairies, but thin and rather scruffy. As she was only a beginner fairy her magic was a disaster, but it never seemed to matter too much.

One day, there was great excitement in the part of Fairyland where she lived because Queen Mab, the queen of the fairies, was coming. Not surprisingly, everyone wanted to put on a good show for her.

"We could do a dance," said Appleblossom.

"I think we should sing," chirped Larkspur.

"What about a play?" said Skipwillow.

"Hmm," said Perriwiggin. "Fairy Nuff, what do you think we should do?"

"Well, how about a bit of everything?" she replied.

"Excellent," said Perriwiggin. "We'll take turns doing whatever we feel Queen Mab would like. But we must keep this visit to ourselves. The hobgoblins would love to spoil it."

The next day, Fairy Nuff met her friend Catkin.

"I'm going to make a picture out of spiders' webs," said Catkin. "What about you?"

"It's a surprise," replied Fairy Nuff. "But I'll be using magic."

"The last time you used magic you turned all the trees into purple piglets by mistake," said Catkin.

"Whoops-a-buttercup," said Fairy Nuff, as she remembered. Then she set about arranging her surprise. She was going to do a spell which would write something in the sky, but what? She wandered along a path trying out some rhyme ideas:

"*Queen Mab, you are welcome,*
Here's some flowers, want to smell some?"

"Hmm, it's a bit long," she thought. Then she stopped and yelled, "*Queen Mab, you are fab* ... Brilliant!"

"What are you doing?" came a voice.

She looked and saw a crow sitting on a branch.

"It's a secret for Queen Mab," she said.

The crow's eyes lit up. "Really? When's she coming then?"

"I'm not allowed to tell you that it's this evening," said Fairy Nuff.

Unfortunately, the crow wasn't really a crow at all. It was Gobby, the chief hobgoblin, who now scrambled down from the tree and ran home, chuckling. The hobgoblins were always looking for ways to annoy the fairies. Very soon, they had thought up a horrible plan to ruin the royal visit.

That evening, Queen Mab arrived in a beautiful water lily coach, which was pulled by dragonflies. The celebrations got underway. Hop-o-my-Thumb played her harp, Larkspur sang a song and Appleblossom danced on a large mushroom. There were many more wonderful things before Skipwillow, Acorncup and Merrywort performed a play about the fairies beating the hobgoblins at football. Everyone gathered around and cheered and clapped so loudly that no one noticed the hobgoblins creeping nearer.

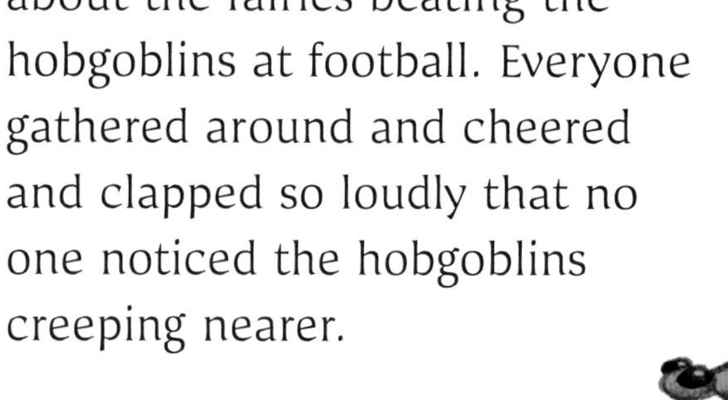

"Come on," whispered Gobby. "We'll hide in the bushes behind this flowerbed. They won't be laughing for long."

There were muffled giggles from the others as they got their smelly-spells ready. These were spells which, when set off by magic, covered whoever was near them with a bright, slimy, gooey stuff which was stinkier than a mountain of old manure.

Back at the celebrations, Fairy Nuff was the last to perform. She leapt into the clearing, but was so excited that she tripped over a molehill. As she hit the ground, the spell shot out of her magic wand. It landed in the flowerbed near the hobgoblins and set everything off like fireworks. Bluebells, dandelions and daisies all whooshed up like rockets, and so did the hobgoblins.

There were great clouds of green, blue, silver, yellow – it was like a sparkling rainbow.

The smelly-spells went so high that the fairies couldn't smell them. But the hobgoblins could. They got covered in stinky stuff and shouted "Euuugh!" and "Phaaaaw!" and "Wheeew!" which from the ground sounded like firework noises. Eventually, all that could be seen in the sky were the words "Queen Mab is fab."

As the hobgoblins slunk off unseen, all scorched and smelly, Queen Mab said, "Thank you, Fairy Nuff. That's the best flowerwork display I've ever seen!"

Fairy Nuff and the goggle monster

One morning, the people of the village of Great Wheezing awoke to a terrible calamity. Julia, the elder daughter of Old Barden, the village gardener, had disappeared. The grown-ups all milled about helplessly, trying to decide what to do (especially P.C. Fleeceman, the village policeman). Only Molly, Julia's little sister, knew what had happened. However, no one would listen to her, so she went to the forest outside the village and started to cry. Her sobs were interrupted by a wild screeching:

"Blue! I said BLUE!"

Molly looked behind a bush and saw a patch of what looked like bluebells, only they were bright red. In front of them was a fairy, waving a magic wand and yelling madly. The fairy was a little thin and rather plain and scruffy.

"Hello," said Molly. "I like your redbells."

The fairy spun around so quickly that she toppled over and dropped her wand, which fizzed madly.

"Whoops-a-buttercup," said the fairy. " Sorry, er, I'm Fairy Nuff."

"I'm Molly," said Molly, and burst into tears again. At this point, any other fairy would have been very cautious, but Fairy Nuff had a heart as kind as a summer's day. She listened as Molly told her all about her sister's disappearance. When she'd finished, Fairy Nuff said, "And you think you saw what happened?"

"I don't *think*, I know," said Molly. "She was grabbed by a huge monster with the most enormous eyes I've ever seen."

"*Goggle-Eyes!*" exclaimed Fairy Nuff. "He's horrible. He lives on a mountain somewhere near Iceland. His big, goggly eyes are special: he never has to go to sleep completely. He can always keep one open, which will make it very difficult to rescue Julia."

"What? Do you mean you'll rescue her?" said Molly.

"Of course," said Fairy Nuff. She didn't tell Molly that as she was a beginner fairy she wasn't supposed to attempt anything dangerous. But then, she was a rebel with a wand. "Let's go!" she said, waving it bravely. "To Iceland!"

After visiting Ireland, then Thailand, they eventually ended up in a cold cave.

"Are we a bit nearer to Goggle-Eyes this time?" said Molly.

"Who said that?" came a deep voice that boomed around the cave.

"Does that answer your question?" whispered Fairy Nuff.

"Aha! Supper!" said Goggle-Eyes. They saw two huge eyes looking at them. Next to him was a cage containing Julia. Fairy Nuff wasn't very quick, but when a monster is about to shake salt and pepper over you, you tend to think rather quickly.

"But we've got something for you," she said. Goggle-Eyes paused. Everyone likes a present, even hungry monsters.

"What is it?" he said.

"Er ... it's a ... erm ..." said Fairy Nuff. Then an idea struck her. "A concert," she said looking at Molly. "My friend Molly here is an amazing musician." Molly looked worried. The only music she ever played was on her CD player.

"Listen," said Fairy Nuff, thinking this spell:

"Play, O music, close both his eyes,
A flute to toot to beddy-byes."

Immediately in Molly's hands there appeared some bagpipes. "Whoops-a-pansy," muttered Fairy Nuff.

Molly began to play the bagpipes and, with the help of the magic, managed quite a good tune.

"Lovely!" said the monster. "It reminds me of Grandpa Goggle MacGoggle. When I was a mini-monster we used to dance before I went to bed." Then the monster got up and jigged around the floor, whooping madly. Far from sending him to sleep, he was so enjoying himself his huge eyes were open wider than ever.

When Molly had run out of breath, the monster said, "Right, now I'll have my supper."

"Is that what you did after you danced with your grandpa?" asked Fairy Nuff.

"Don't be stupid," said Goggle-Eyes. "It was bedtime, he used to tell me a story."

"Well that's your second surprise," said Fairy Nuff and immediately launched into a story. "Once upon a time, in a far-away land ..."

"Is it about Baby Goggle?" the monster interrupted.

"... Lived Baby Goggle," said the quick-thinking fairy. And she went on to tell a fantastic story in which Baby Goggle terrorized three whole villages and barbecued all their sheep. When she'd finished, there was loud snoring.

Fairy Nuff had worked an amazing trick. As the monster's eyes had been open incredibly wide during all the frantic music and dancing, they were now incredibly tired. So he had closed both of them for a quick nap.

Julia was rescued from the cage and, after two tries, Fairy Nuff managed to magic them all back to Great Wheezing. The delighted villagers held a huge party that evening, at which Fairy Nuff was the special guest. Just as she was about to make her speech, a messenger arrived from Queen Mab, the queen of the fairies.

"Attention!" he said. "Queen Mab says that Fairy Nuff is no longer a beginner fairy. She will be responsible for looking after this village from now on." There was a huge cheer, especially from Molly and Julia.

Fairy Nuff stood on the table and said, "You don't need to worry any more about Goggle-Eyes. He'll be so embarrassed that he won't dare show up around here again. Still, to be on the safe side, you'd better keep your eyes open."

The vinegar bottle woman

Once there was a woman called Mrs. Funnybones, who lived in a vinegar bottle. One day, a fairy was fluttering past the bottle when she heard Mrs. Funnybones talking and muttering to herself.

"Dear-oh-dearie me," she moaned. "Fancy me living in a mere vinegar bottle. I ought to live in a pretty little cottage with a thatched roof and roses around the front door."

The fairy, who was called Skip, was a kind creature. She listened to Mrs. Funnybones' complaints, and then she said,

"Just shout 'Wazoomer!', blink your eyes,
Tomorrow morning, big surprise."

Then she vanished in a cloud of fairy dust.

Mrs. Funnybones did as she was told, and the next morning she awoke in the prettiest little cottage you could imagine. She rushed outside and admired the thatched roof and the roses around the front door. Mrs. Funnybones was very happy in her little cottage. Every morning she went into her garden to smile at the rising sun. She also kept a hen, which laid a fresh egg every day for her breakfast.

Some time later, Skip the fairy decided to look in on Mrs. Funnybones to make sure everything was all right. When she got there, Mrs. Funnybones started complaining again.

"Dear-oh-dearie me. Fancy me living in a mere cottage. I ought to live in a house on a busy street, with people passing by and admiring the big, brass door knocker."

Skip listened patiently, then said,

"Just shout 'Wazoomer!', blink your eyes,
Tomorrow morning, big surprise."

Mrs. Funnybones did as she was told, and in the morning she found herself in a bigger bed, in a bigger house. Through the open window she heard a passer-by say,

"Wow! Look at that amazing big, brass door knocker!"

She loved her house, and she kept it clean and tidy. People on her street often stopped by for tea. She walked to the supermarket every day and bought eggs, bread and orange juice for her breakfast.

Some time later Skip was passing by the house again, when she heard Mrs. Funnybones' voice saying,

"Dear-oh-dearie me. Fancy me living in a mere house. I ought to be living in a mansion with a lake in the garden."

Again, Skip listened, then said,

"Just shout 'Wazoomer!', blink your eyes,
Tomorrow morning, big surprise."

Sure enough, Mrs. Funnybones awoke the next morning in a beautiful four-poster bed, in a huge mansion. She had a large garden with a lake. She also had eggs, bread, mushrooms, tomatoes, bacon and sausages, delivered every day for her breakfast.

Skip was sure that this time Mrs. Funnybones would by happy, but no! Not long after, as she was flying through the mansion garden, she heard a sad voice from the edge of the lake.

"Dear-oh-dearie me. Fancy me living in a mere mansion. I ought to live in a palace and be a queen, with lots of servants." Skip couldn't believe her ears. But her disbelief wasn't as great as her kindness, so she said,

"Just shout 'Wazoomer!', blink your eyes,
Tomorrow morning, big surprise."

Mrs. Funnybones became Queen Mrs. Funnybones. She did lots of queenie things, such as open buildings, launch ships, meet important visitors and travel to foreign lands.

She also had servants to bring her breakfast in bed: orange juice, eggs, bread, mushrooms, tomatoes, bacon and sausages.

A short while later, flitting past the palace, Skip heard something which almost made her wings wither.

"Dear-oh-dearie me. Fancy me being a mere queen of one country. I ought to be the Ruler of the World."

Skip sighed and said again, (altogether now),

"Just shout 'Wazoomer!', blink your eyes,
Tomorrow morning, big surprise."

When she awoke next morning, Mrs. Funnybones had the biggest surprise of all. She was back in her vinegar bottle. It was exactly the same, except for a small globe Skip had put there so Mrs. Funnybones could rule over the world to her heart's content.

The nose tree

Wendy held on to the stolen doughnut, ran deep into the wood, and sat down. Something stirred nearby, and, to her great surprise, she saw it was a sleeping fairy. Instantly, she forgot about the doughnut and carefully caught the fairy by the arm, waking her up.

"Oh no," said the little creature. "I must learn not to go to sleep outside Fairyland." She started to cry, so Wendy took pity on her and released her grip.

The fairy stopped crying and said, "At least I'm not as silly as you. If you'd held on to me for a week, I would have had to grant you any wish you liked." It was now Wendy's turn to cry. She was very poor, and a fairy wish would have been very welcome.

"Oh, all right," said the fairy. "I will give you something after all."

The fairy waved her hand, and Wendy's doughnut moved all by itself, became a silver bracelet and slipped itself over her wrist.

"It glows when magic's around," said the fairy, and she vanished.

A few days later, Wendy's travels took her to a large city. Everyone was lining the main street. After a while, a procession came along.

"That's lucky, I've come on a carnival day," said, Wendy to a woman nearby.

"We do this every day," she groaned. "It's Prince Handsome. We all have to look at him. Mind you do."

As the procession came close, Wendy saw a man in an elegant coach. He certainly was handsome, and he knew it, because he was looking at himself in a golden mirror. Just then, Wendy noticed a doughnut in the road, about to be squashed. As she bent to pick it up, she heard a thin but stern voice.

"Stop! There's someone who is not looking at my radiant beauty," said the prince.

"Guards! Arrest her at once!" he said.

Wendy was taken back to the palace and left alone in a room. After a while, she noticed that her bracelet was glowing. It got brighter as she moved closer to a cupboard. Wendy looked inside and saw the fairy who had given her the bracelet. She was in a glass box with a huge padlock.

"I fell asleep again," said the fairy. "The prince caught me. In a few more days he'll have a wish."

"What will he wish for?" asked Wendy.

It was the prince himself who answered her, "To rule the world!" His eyes were bright with power-craziness.

"I will wish that everyone in the world must adore my wondrousness, and be my slaves forever."

Wendy knew that she must get away from the castle, so she said, "Beware, Prince. See my bracelet glowing! Its magic powers will spoil your plan." At this, the prince thought it would be best if she wasn't around any longer.

"You may go, but if I ever see you again, I'll send you to prison for a thousand years."

Once away from the city, Wendy wandered around the forest until she noticed that her bracelet was glowing again. She looked up and saw a strange-looking tree, heavy with huge, shiny apples. She ate one, and her nose grew to an enormous length.

"Thanks, bracelet," she said with a huff. It was still glowing, and she saw that next to the apple tree was a pear tree. "Oh well, I'll try these," she said. "Who knows, they may give me ears as big as parachutes." She ate a pear, and her nose grew back to the normal size again. Then, she had a brilliant idea.

Disguising herself as an old woman, Wendy went back to the city with a basket of magic apples. Just before the prince's procession, she put the basket on the roadside. The people were so busy looking at the prince they didn't see it, but he did.

"What splendiferous apples," he said. "I can see my gorgeous face in them, so they must be pretty amazing. Bring them to the palace for my lunch."

Back in the forest, Wendy put some pears into a bag and, still disguised, went back to the city.

At the castle, Wendy amazed the guards by knowing there was something wrong with the prince. She said she was the only doctor who could cure him. The courtyard where the prince had eaten the apples was now full of his nose.

"My magnificent looks! Ruined!" he wailed.

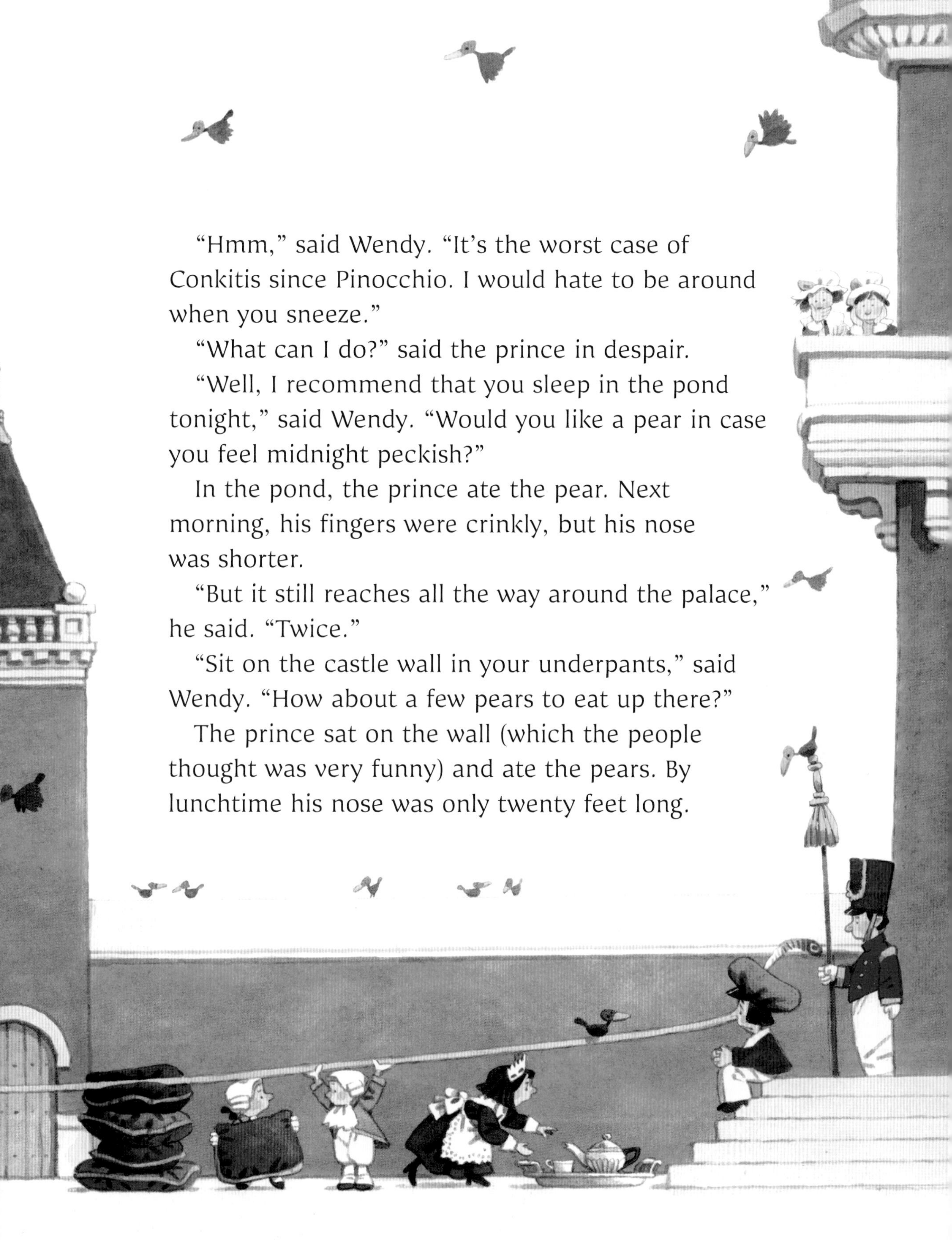

"Hmm," said Wendy. "It's the worst case of Conkitis since Pinocchio. I would hate to be around when you sneeze."

"What can I do?" said the prince in despair.

"Well, I recommend that you sleep in the pond tonight," said Wendy. "Would you like a pear in case you feel midnight peckish?"

In the pond, the prince ate the pear. Next morning, his fingers were crinkly, but his nose was shorter.

"But it still reaches all the way around the palace," he said. "Twice."

"Sit on the castle wall in your underpants," said Wendy. "How about a few pears to eat up there?"

The prince sat on the wall (which the people thought was very funny) and ate the pears. By lunchtime his nose was only twenty feet long.

"Shall I stay longer?" he said. "My bottom's a bit cold, but I don't mind."

"No," said Wendy. "There is only one way to get your nose finally back to size."

"How?" he said. "I'll do anything, anything at all."

"Release the fairy," said Wendy.

"But I want to rule the world," he said.

"With a twenty foot nose?" said Wendy.

Prince Handsome released the fairy.

"I shall make your nose the right size," she said. "But if you ever say how good-looking you are, it will grow to super-elephant proportions again."

Then she looked at Wendy. "Thank you very much. Enjoy your doughnut." She disappeared.

Wendy noticed that her bracelet had fallen to the floor and was now a doughnut again.

"I bet it's a magic one," said Prince Handsome.

Wendy ate half of it and, as she swallowed, the doughnut grew back so that it was whole again.

"It's a never-ending one," she said. "How clever of you to know. You must have a nose for magic."

Crafty Herbert

Strange things sometimes happened in the village of Bomford. Once, a park bench had suddenly turned into a huge chocolate ice cream, which wasn't very pleasant for the person sitting on it at the time. It was always Crafty Herbert's fault.

Crafty Herbert was a particular type of fairy, known as a shape-shifter. This meant he could become anything he wanted in the blink of an eye.

On the edge of the village lived a woman named Nancy. She had a small cottage with a garden as pretty as a box of paints. She spoke kindly to the flowers and always watered them well. This pleased the fairies, who made sure that the flowers lasted an extra-long time.

Crafty Herbert was not pleased though. He got fed up with hearing the fairies chattering about how sweet Nancy was, always so cheerful and kind. So he set out to do something about it.

One day, Nancy went to milk her cow, called Moo. She didn't know that Crafty Herbert had hidden her cow and turned himself into one exactly the same.

"Hello Moo my darling," said Nancy, sitting on her stool and putting her bucket underneath the cow's udder. She was just about to start milking when the cow walked forward.

"What are you doing?" asked Nancy, moving her stool and bucket. But as she sat down the cow stepped back to where it was at the beginning. Normally, it took Nancy half an hour to milk Moo. Today, it took three hours.

"Well, I'll be a marmalade milk-churn, what's come over you?" she said, picking up the bucket.

"Well, I know what's going to come over you," thought Crafty Herbert, and he kicked the bucket in Nancy's hand so that the milk went all over her.

Nancy was speechless with rage. She turned and walked briskly back to her house, hardly noticing the muffled sound of mooey laughter.

Tricks such as this went on for weeks, until Nancy could stand it no more. She went to see the Wise Woman, who lived in a cave just outside the village.

When Nancy had finished telling her tale, the Wise Woman said, “It’s old Crafty Herbert. I’m as sure as ducks are quackers.” And she told Nancy all about the fairy and his shape-shifting tricks. “He’s like magic clay,” she said.

“But how can I stop him?” said Nancy.

“He only plays tricks when he knows it’s annoying someone. He hates all laughter but his own,” said the Wise Woman. “So, beat him at his own game.”

Nancy spent all of the next day working in her strawberry patch. She was just bending down to pull up some weeds underneath the scarecrow, when the scarecrow (who was really you-know-who) turned into a bag of flour, which burst all over poor Nancy. Her first reaction was to scream with rage, but then she remembered what the Wise Woman had said and roared with laughter.

"Another wonderful trick!" she guffawed.

Crafty Herbert, who had been running away disguised as a puff of wind, suddenly stopped. He looked at Nancy and her laughing face, and he started to scowl.

"Wonderful tricks? Aren't you angry then?" he asked.

"Angry? They've made my life so full of surprises, I never know what's coming next."

Crafty Herbert was just going off in a sulk when something made him stop. Two boys from another village were passing and had watched Nancy speaking. As Herbert was disguised as a puff of wind, they'd thought Nancy was talking to herself.

"Look at that silly old woman, Gary," said one.

"She's talking to thin air, Barry," said the other. "And she's covered in flour. She's so stupid, she wouldn't notice if we took her strawberries."

They pushed their way into the garden and started to stuff their pockets with fruit.

Now Crafty Herbert was naughty, but he wasn't nasty like these louts. When they weren't looking, he turned himself into two beautiful girls.

"Hello Mother, hello boys," said one.

The boys stared, with their mouths open so wide that the strawberry juice ran down their chins. Nancy was speechless.

"Would you like to come to the fair with us?" said the other, with a smile. Then the girls turned and walked out of the front gate, beckoning to the boggle-eyed bullies. The boys forgot the strawberries and fell over each other to get at the gate. They walked with the girls for ages until eventually it began to get dark.

"It's just across this field," said the girls, opening a gate. The boys leapt over the wall to show off, and instantly sunk up to their waists in a slimy, wet bog.

The girls each grabbed a boy and started to pull.

When the boys were nearly out, a very strange thing happened. The girls began to merge together. Then before you could say "soggy underpants" each boy found himself holding a hand of Crafty Herbert, who began to laugh loudly. The boys were absolutely scared out of their wits.

"It's a ghost, Gary!" cried Barry.

"It's a monster, Barry!" cried Gary.

"RUN!" they cried together.

They scampered off in opposite directions, and didn't find each other for three months.

As for Nancy, she lived quietly and happily in her little cottage, and quite undisturbed by mischievous fairies, for the rest of her days.

The little red hen

In a small cottage there lived a pig, a cat, a duck and a little red hen. The little red hen was a busy red hen who spent all day cleaning the house, polishing the windows and tidying the garden. The other three animals never did any work at all.

One day, the little red hen found a grain of corn. "Who will help me plant this grain of corn?" she asked.

"Not I," said the pig, with a grunt and a sigh.

"Not I," purred the cat, lying down on the mat.

"Not I," said the duck on the pond, with a "quack."

So the little red hen planted the grain of corn all by herself.

All through the spring and summer the grain grew until it ripened into a golden ear of corn. Then the little red hen knew that it was harvest time.

"Who will help me harvest the corn?" she asked.
"Not I," grunted the pig, with the laziest sigh.
"Not I," purred the cat, from her comfortable mat.
"Not I," said the duck, with a splash and a "quack."

So the little red hen harvested the corn all by herself, pecking at the stalk until it fell over. Then she separated the grains from the husks and carefully placed them in a handkerchief – all except for four, which she saved in a drawer.

"Who will help me take the corn to be ground into flour?" she then asked.

"Not I," said the pig from his mud, with a sigh.
"Not I," purred the cat, all curled up on the mat.
"Not I," said the duck, swimming by with a "quack."

So the little red hen took the grains of corn to the miller all by herself, and asked him to grind them into flour.

After a few days, a small bag of flour was delivered to the cottage where the animals lived.

"Oh good," said the little red hen. Then she shouted, "Who will help me make the flour into bread?"

"Not I," said the pig. "I'm asleep in my sty."

"Not I," purred the cat. "I'm asleep on my mat."

"Not I," said the duck with an extra loud "quack."

"All right," sighed the little red hen, "I shall have to make it all by myself." She went into the kitchen, poured the flour on to the table, added some water and yeast, then kneaded the mixture into a dough. When the dough had risen, she popped it into the oven to bake.

Soon the smell of fresh bread wafted through the house, into the garden, and even to the pond.

When it reached the pig, he wrinkled his snout and all of a sudden felt very hungry. So he heaved himself out of the mud, and trotted into the house. Behind him was the cat, and behind her was the duck.

They arrived in the kitchen just in time to see the little red hen open the oven door. Inside was the tastiest looking loaf of bread that any of them had ever seen.

"Now, who is going to help me eat my bread?" asked the little red hen.

"Me!" said the pig, fairly grunting with glee.

"And me!" purred the cat. "It's time for my tea."

"And me!" said the duck with a waddle and "quack."

"Tough luck!" replied the hen. "All this work has made me so hungry that I'm going to eat it all by myself. But I'll tell you how you can get some more bread."

"How?" they said, eagerly. And the little red hen took out from the drawer three of the four grains of corn she had saved, and gave one to each of the other animals.

"Get planting!" said the hen. The pig, the cat and the duck went out to plant their grains. "I'll plant mine when I've eaten," thought the hen. Then she sat and ate her bread – every last crumb.

Button nose

An old woman was sitting in her chair by a crackling evening fire. She was just dozing off, when the door burst open and in rushed her granddaughter.

"Hello Grandma!" yelled the girl. Then she ran excitedly over to the old woman and gave her a hug.

"How was your trip?" asked the old woman.

"Great, thanks. We went to a place called Lillia, and do you know what? On the day we left everyone was walking around with their fingers ..."

"Pressing their noses flat, like buttons?" the old woman said, finishing the sentence.

"Yes!" said the girl. "How did you know?"

The old woman sighed. The glow from the fire was just bright enough to see the sparkle in her eyes as she told her granddaughter this story ...

Long ago in the land of Lillia there was a poor peasant and his wife. When they had been married for only a year, she had a son. He was a pretty child, but as he was growing up, his parents realized that there was one part of him that wasn't growing: his nose. It remained small, round and pink – just like a button. The other children would run after him calling, "Button Nose, Button Nose!" This made him sad, because he longed to be friends with the children and join in their games.

One day, when Button Nose was quite big (except for his nose, of course), a dreadful thing happened. A wicked witch called Witch Hazel cast a spell on the King and Queen of Lillia, banishing them to the top of a glass tower. No one was able to rescue them because the tower was impossible to climb.

Witch Hazel became the ruler of Lillia, and everyone was afraid. From that moment no birds sang, the flowers all died, and everyone spoke in whispers and never smiled. Poor Button Nose worked in the palace, doing all the nasty jobs such as chasing rats from the kitchen, fetching wood from the cellar and cleaning the toilets.

One evening, Button Nose heard a great howling and wailing coming from the dining hall. He went to investigate, and found that the noise was being made by the witch who was singing. As it was her birthday, she was celebrating, and had drunk three bottles of wine. Feeling nervous and swallowing hard, Button Nose wished the witch a happy birthday.

"You're rrrright!" croaked the witch. "It is happy. I am the queen of all the land, and no one can take that away from me."

Button Nose suddenly felt brave, and said, "You must be very clever Queen Witch Hazel, because no one can find a way to break your spell and free the old king and queen."

"Of course not. How could they know that the only way to break it is to show me something that no one has ever seen before?" replied the witch. "Even if they did know, they'd never find anything because as soon as they found it, they would see it – so when I saw it, it would have been seen before ... see?" The witch cackled and began to sing again. It was so loud that the windows rattled and the cat darted under the stairs and put its paws over its ears.

Poor Button Nose spent a restless night. If only he could think of something that no one had ever seen before.

The next day, he told the witch there were some people outside with presents for her. In spite of a bad headache, she became very excited, and put on a large ruby crown that she'd found in the jewel cupboard.

"Summon the present bearers!" she said, in as regal a voice as she could manage.

The door opened and in came the royal gamekeeper, carrying a silver plate on which was a magnificent fish. Its scales shimmered red, then blue, then green – and its tail was silver, like moonshine.

Button Nose, his knees knocking, said, "I bet no one has ever seen the like of this before."

"Don't be silly," said the witch sharply. "The old fool saw it himself when he caught it." Then she turned on Button Nose. "Did you really think I'd be fooled by your sneaky trick?"

"Er, no, your majesty, whatever gave you that idea?" he said, trying not to turn red. Then thinking quickly, he added, "I have a present for you, too."

"Oh?" said the witch, raising an eyebrow.

"Your Majesty, I would like to give you this!" And Button Nose produced a plate on which was a shiny green apple and a knife.

"An apple?" shouted the witch. "What sort of present is that for a Royal Person such as me?"

"Just have a look inside, your Highness," begged Button Nose. "Then you'll get a big surprise."

Witch Hazel sat down. She thought that there might be a jewel hidden in the apple, so she snatched up the knife, sliced the apple down the middle and peered at the two halves.

"Why, you little beast, there's nothing here!" said the witch.

In a flash there was nothing of her either. She vanished in a puff of smoke, and in her place sat the king and queen. The magic spell had been broken because the witch had looked at the inside of the apple, which no one had ever seen before.

The king and queen were so grateful to Button Nose that they promoted him to head butler. To celebrate, they ordered that every year, on his birthday, everyone should keep their noses pressed flat – as flat as a button.

Nail soup

One winter evening, just as the sun was going down, a beggar knocked at the door of a cottage and asked for shelter.

"Oh, all right," grumbled the old woman who lived in the cottage. "Don't expect any food, though, because my cupboard's as bare as a baby's bottom."

The beggar sat by the weak fire feeling cold and hungry. Then he had an idea. Smiling, he took an old nail from his pocket.

"This here's a magic nail," he said. "Last night it made the best nail soup I have ever tasted."

"Nail soup? I've never heard anything so stupid in all my born days," said the woman with a scowl.

"It's true," the beggar continued. "All I did was to boil it in a saucepan. Do you want to try some?"

Although the old woman was far from convinced, she decided she would play along. "Go on then," she said. "But you'll have to show me how to do it."

"Right. First we need a cooking pot half full of water," said the beggar. The old woman brought one, and the tramp put it on the stove. Then he dropped in the nail and said,

"Nail we trust that all your rust,
Will make a tasty soup for us."

Then he sat down and waited. After a while the woman became curious and peeked into the pot.

"Last night I added some salt and pepper. It made an ordinary soup, into a good soup," said the beggar.

So the old woman went to her cupboard, got the salt and pepper and put some into the pot. After a few more minutes, she looked in the pot again.

"Pity you don't have any food," said the beggar stroking his chin. "A single onion would make a good soup, very good."

"I'm sure I could find one," said the woman, her curiosity growing stronger. She went and looked in her cupboard. As she opened the door, the beggar saw that inside the shelves were groaning under the weight of all kinds of food.

"Why, you mean old thing," thought the beggar.

He stood for a while, silently stirring the onion into the soup. Then he said, "Shame you don't have any carrots and potatoes to go with the onion, or a parsnip. They would make a very good soup extremely good."

The woman was now feeling pretty hungry, and she disappeared again into the cupboard. She emerged with an armful of fresh vegetables, which she peeled and chopped. The beggar put them into the pot.

"This is coming along nicely," said the beggar. "But I tell you what."

"What?" said the woman, her tummy rumbling like distant thunder.

"Some tender, lean meat would make an extremely good soup, amazingly good." The woman fairly ran to the cupboard and came back with a huge piece of steak which she cut up and gave to the beggar to pop into the pot.

By now, the soup was beginning to smell delicious. The beggar said, "Pity to have to eat such an amazingly good soup at such a boringly bare table. I always think food tastes better when a table is properly laid, don't you?"

"Of course," said the woman. Not wanting to spoil the soup, she brought her best tablecloth and spread it on the table. Then she got out china soup bowls and shiny silver spoons, even some candlesticks with candles in them.

The beggar stirred the soup for a bit longer, then he said, “Shame you have no food in the house, because some bread would make an amazingly good soup, simply soooper.” Again the woman ran to the cupboard, this time bringing a loaf of bread that she had baked that morning.

Finally, the beggar sighed and shook his head.

“What’s the matter?” said the woman, her mouth watering at the smell of the soup.

“I was just thinking that it’s a pity we can’t have any wine with the soup, wine would make a ... ”

But the woman wasn’t listening. “I’m sure I’ve got some somewhere,” she said rushing into her cellar. She brought back a fine-looking old bottle, and two of her best glasses.

“Now, I think the soup is ready,” said the beggar, carefully removing the nail and putting it back in his pocket. Then they sat down at the table and had an absolute feast.

After she had finished, the old woman declared it was the best soup she had ever tasted. Then she offered the beggar cheese, apple pie and chocolates to thank him, which they washed down with another bottle of wine.

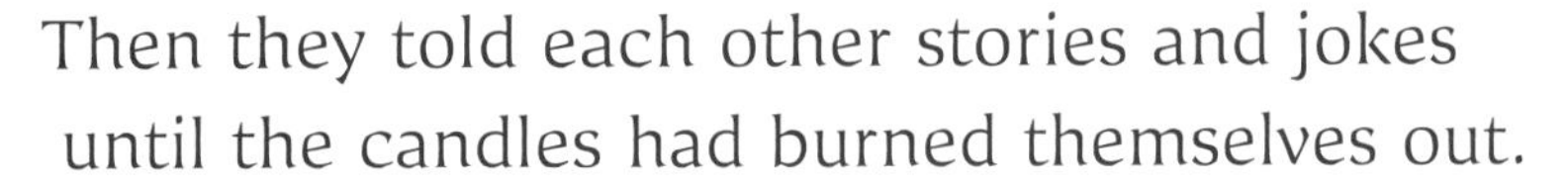

Then they told each other stories and jokes until the candles had burned themselves out.

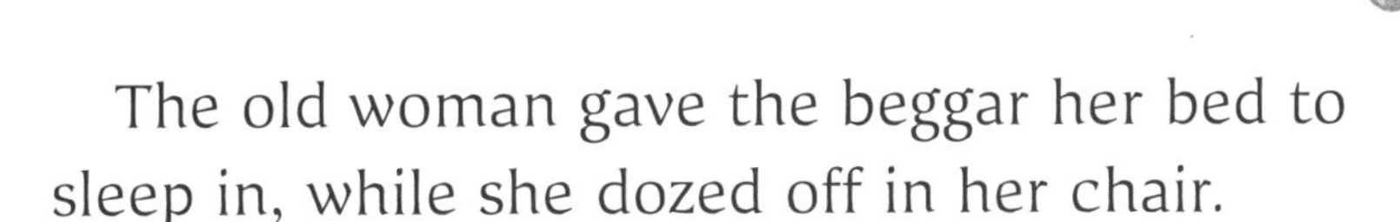

The old woman gave the beggar her bed to sleep in, while she dozed off in her chair.

And there are no prizes for guessing what they dreamed about: the simply sooooper nail soup.

Dragon train

Once there was a town called Wibblington. Next to this town was a mountain, and on this mountain lived a friendly dragon called Frazzlenose, who loved steam trains. It might have been because they puffed out smoke rather like he did; or because they carried lots of the food he liked best – coal. The fact remained that he was never happier than when he was flying along next to a train – especially, the Wibblington Express.

The trouble was, the people on the train didn't know that Frazzlenose was a kind dragon. Every time he appeared they screamed, "It's a dragon! Quick, hide! He'll sizzle us to a crisp with his breath!"

So Frazzlenose had to be content with following the train from high up in the sky, out of sight of the nervous passengers.

Wibblington was in a large country, governed by a large queen called Good Queen Daisy. It was her custom, every New Year's Day, to choose a town in her queendom for a special royal visit. The town would then be known as The Royal Town for the whole year, and receive a gold statue of the queen. It was the greatest thing a town could wish for.

One day, while the people of Wibblington were going about their normal business, a messenger galloped into the market square on his horse.

"Hear ye! Hear ye!" he proclaimed in a loud voice to the people, who were quickly gathering around. "Know ye that, thanks to the kindness of Her Royal Highness Good Queen Daisy, the humble town of Wibblington will be humble no more ..."

"Get to the point, will you!" interrupted a man.

"Yes, it's freezing standing around here!" said a woman. The crowd grumbled in agreement.

The messenger put down his scroll, sighed and said, "You're going to be the next Royal Town."

"Hooray! Hoorah! Hoo-wibble!" shouted the people. Then they pulled the man from his horse and gave him a plateful of peanut butter sandwiches and a huge mug of tea. The horse got a bucket of oats.

"The queen will arrive on New Year's Day to make the official announcement," said the messenger between mouthfuls. Then he finished his tea with a big slurp, climbed on to his horse and rode back down the road, hiccupping loudly as he went.

During the next few days the people were very busy. The town was tidied, swept, cleaned, scrubbed and polished ready for the royal visit.

Pillar boxes gleamed, lamp-posts sparkled, and you could see your face in the cobblestones. The train was also cleaned, for on the morning of New Year's Day it would leave to pick up the queen from her palace.

At last, New Year's Day arrived. The train was given a last minute polish, and the red carpet was laid out ready for when it returned carrying the Most Important Person. The people scrambled on board, and were so excited that they didn't really notice that snow was beginning to fall. The Wibblington Express puffed out of the station and began the journey to the palace. Frazzlenose followed at a safe distance. The snow continued to fall.

By the time the train reached the palace, the snow was almost as high as the funnel. The queen's royal carriage was joined on to the rest of the train, and all was ready for the return journey. But despite a lot of huffing and puffing, and a good bit of chuffing, the train stayed absolutely still. It was stuck in the snow.

"Oh dear," said the queen. "What a to-do. I can't possibly get to Wibblington today. I shall have to find another, closer town. I'm very sorry."

The people were overcome with disappointment. Some of them shed tears, others just looked out of the window at the still-falling snow, thinking that it was unlikely they would be chosen again. Even the train looked sad.

Suddenly, from the gloomy snowy clouds, came a whooshing of wings and a crackle of fiery breath. "It's the dragon!" shouted the people. "As if things weren't bad enough, now he's come to finish us off." They put their hands over their heads and prepared to be burned to a cinder.

The next thing they knew, the train was moving.

They looked out of the windows and saw something quite astonishing. Sitting on the front of the train, breathing all the fire he could muster, was Frazzlenose.

As he breathed, the snow on the tracks melted, and the train was slowly able to head for home.

The people cheered with all their voices, "Three cheers for ... what's the dragon's name?"

"Frazzlenose," shouted Frazzlenose, between hot snorts.

"Three cheers for Frazzlenose! Hip-hip hoo-wibble!" they chorused. Even the queen joined in.

The train got back to Wibblington and the celebrations began. Good Queen Daisy made a speech, they all ate the biggest banquet the town had ever produced – and who do you think the special guest was?

Frazzlenose, of course. He sat at the queen's table wearing the train driver's hat and crunching away at his plate of coal.

After that, Frazzlenose was allowed to travel on the train whenever he wanted to. He was even allowed into the cab provided he promised not to eat all the coal. He was very useful when the engine needed an extra blast of fire on really steep hills.

When the gold statue arrived from the queen, on it were written the words:

"To The Royal Town of Wibblington
and its Dragon Train."

The princess and the pea

Long ago, there was a land where the mountains were capped with snow, the pastures were rich and green and the people were happy. In this land there lived a prince who was so handsome, so friendly and so kind that every girl in the land fell in love with him. But the prince was so fussy that he only wanted to marry a princess, a real princess.

He journeyed far and wide looking for his ideal princess, but there was always something wrong. Either they were too tall for him, or too short, or they were too grumpy and never smiled. After many months of searching, the prince came home and said to the king and queen, "It's no good, I can't find a princess I like enough to marry. I shall have to live alone to the end of my days."

A week later, the castle was in the grip of a ferocious blizzard. Snow beat against the windows and whistled into every crack it could find. In the middle of the night there came a timid knock at the door.

The king got out of bed. "Who can that be on a night like this?" he asked. He went downstairs and shuffled across the hall. Yawning, he opened the door a little, and in the light that spilled out into the night, he saw a girl. She was shivering with cold and half covered in snow.

"You poor dear," said the king. "Come on in and warm yourself by the fire."

"Th-th-thank you," said the girl, hardly able to keep her teeth from chattering. She went and sat by the palace fire, whilst the king warmed up some milk for her. By this time the queen and the prince had also joined them.

"I was looking for the palace, but it was much further than I thought," said the girl, whom the prince thought quite pretty. "You see, I'm a princess." The prince's eyes widened, and his heart beat faster.

The queen knew exactly what her son was thinking, but she thought the girl was probably only pretending to be a princess. She asked her to stay the night so that she could set a trap for her.

While the girl was having a good splash in a hot bath, the queen went to prepare her bedroom. First she placed a dried pea under the mattress of the bed. Then she sent two maids to all the other bedrooms in the palace to find extra mattresses and eiderdowns. Altogether they collected twenty of each. They piled them up on top of each other – first the mattresses, then the eiderdowns – until they almost reached the ceiling.

When the girl was ready for bed, she had to climb a long ladder to get into it.

"Nightie-night," said the queen. Then she added in a low voice, "In the morning we shall know whether you are a real princess."

The next morning at breakfast, the queen asked the girl if she had slept well.

"You have been very kind to me," she replied, a little uneasily. "I don't want to sound ungrateful, but I couldn't sleep a wink because I could feel something small and hard in my bed." Seeing the king, the queen and the prince smiling broadly at each other, the girl added crossly, "Well I don't know why you're all so happy – I'm as bruised as an old apple now."

"We're smiling because in order to feel something as small as a pea through all those soft layers you must be a real princess," said the prince. "Err ... will you marry me?"

The girl's frown turned into a huge grin, and she threw herself into the prince's arms.

The prince and princess lived happily together for many years. They had seven children, who were all given names that began with a "P", because that's how their love had begun – with a pea.

The squire's bride

There was once an old squire who was very rich. His pockets bulged with his money, and his waistcoat bulged with his fat, overfed stomach. He lived in a huge house, and owned all the land as far as the eye could see. In fact he had everything a man might want; everything, that is, except a wife. So he set out to find one.

"I am so rich, I can choose whoever I want," he told his dog. "They will be lining up to marry me."

One day the old squire was admiring his fields of golden corn, when he spotted the farmer's daughter.

"Ho-ho!" he exclaimed. "I can see a wife to be. So young! So strong!" Then his eyes narrowed with greed, "And she will save me money when she's my wife because I won't have to pay her to work." So he invited the girl to his mansion that afternoon.

When she arrived he said pompously, "I have news for you. I have decided to get married, and I have chosen you to be my wife."

"Have you now?" said the farmer's daughter. "Well I've got news for you an' all, I don't want to get wed. And even if I did, you'd be the last person I'd choose."

The squire couldn't believe his ears. "But ... but ... you must be joking!" he said.

"Do you see me laughing?" she replied. "My answer is 'no', and it will stay 'no' until cows lay eggs and pigs fly!" Before he could say another word, she jumped up and marched out of the house.

The squire's face grew bright red, and stamping his foot with rage, he sent for the farmer.

"That girl of yours is as stubborn as a lazy old donkey!" he roared. "I'll tell you what: if you can get her to marry me I'll never charge you another rent." Then the squire pointed out of the window. "And what's more, you can have that meadow, the one full of poppies and daisies."

Now the farmer had wanted that meadow for many a long year – and no more rent either! So he said, "Well, sir, that foolish daughter of mine has never known what's best for her. Maybe if we put our heads together, we could come up with a plan that would please everybody."

So that is what they did, and this was the plan they made. The squire would arrange the wedding, with guests, cake, and a beautiful dress at the ready. Then, on the wedding day, the farmer would tell his daughter that she was wanted for work at the big house. They were sure that when she arrived and saw everyone assembled for the wedding, she would be too afraid to say "No."

Some weeks later, on the wedding day, the squire called his stable boy and ordered, "Go quickly to the farmer and fetch what he has promised me."

Off ran the stable boy, and meeting the farmer on the road said, "Please, sir, I've come to fetch what you promised the squire."

"Oh, aye," replied the farmer with a smile. "She's down in the meadow." The stable boy ran off again and soon arrived at the meadow where the farmer's daughter was busy raking hay.

"Miss," he panted, "I've come to fetch what your father promised the squire."

The girl realized at once what the two men were up to. So, pointing at the old white mare nibbling the grass nearby, she said, "There she is, take her."

The stable boy leapt on to the mare and galloped back to the squire's mansion as fast as possible – which wasn't very fast as the mare was very old. Then he called up to the squire's window, "Excuse me your squireship, I've brought her. She's down here."

"Well done," said the squire, thinking the boy had brought the farmer's daughter. "Take her upstairs to my mother's old room."

"But, sir ..." cried the stable boy.

"No buts, boy. Just do as I say, at once!" bellowed the squire.

It wasn't at all easy persuading the mare to climb the stairs. The stable boy pushed and groaned, and the other servants shoved and grunted. This went on for over an hour, until at last, they succeeded in getting her into the bedroom.

"We've done it!" called the stable boy. "Isn't she stubborn!"

"Oh yes, she certainly is," replied the squire. "Now, quickly fetch the maids and dress her in the wedding gown, there's no time to lose."

The stable boy could hardly believe his ears, but carried out the squire's orders all the same. The maids shrieked and giggled as they tugged at the dress to pull it over the mare's bottom.

Finally, they set the wedding veil between her ears.

"She's ready!" called the boy again.

"Well, bring her downstairs, open the door and announce the bride to all my guests," replied the squire, checking his hair in a mirror.

"Ok, sir," said the boy. With lots of bumps and thumps, the old white mare was brought downstairs. The boy threw open the front door and all the guests who were gathered in the garden turned to view the squire's bride. There stood the mare with her veil all crooked, munching the bridal bouquet.

After a few seconds of stunned silence, the guests, the maids and the stable boy began to laugh loudly. This frightened the poor old mare so much that she galloped off back to the peace and quiet of her meadow. As for the squire, he was so taken aback that he sat down on his hat, and squashed it flat.

In a far-off field the farmer's daughter sang as she worked. As she sang she thought about her future, which featured no squires at all.

The king and his three children

A long time ago in a land far away there lived an old king with three children. They were called Prince Crispin, Prince Horace and Princess Emily. He loved them all dearly, but he knew that he had to choose one to be the next king or queen. As he got older, the king worried about this more and more. It kept him awake at night. "Who would make the best ruler?" he'd ask his teddy bear.

Then one morning he woke up with an idea. He called his children into his throne room, and said, "Now you know that I love you all." They nodded. "But I can only choose one of you to rule when I die. So I am going to give you a test." He reached into his pocket. "Here is a gold coin for each of you. Whoever can use it to fill the palace from top to bottom will be the next king or queen."

Although this worried the royal children, as the palace had seventy-five rooms and miles of passages, they decided the test was a fair one. So each set off in search of something that would fill it.

Prince Crispin went to sit in the palace garden to ponder. On a tree nearby, he saw a bird building its nest with twigs and feathers.

"That's it!" he cried. "Feathers! With my gold coin I could buy millions of feathers, they'll easily fill the palace." So off he went to see the man who made feather beds.

"How many feathers would you sell me for this gold coin?" asked Prince Crispin.

The feather bed man's eyes grew wide at the sight of the gold. "Five wagon loads," he replied.

"Agreed!" said Prince Crispin. And soon he was riding back to the palace with five wagons and a big smile.

Prince Horace went to the market. He looked around at the rolls of cloth, jars of jam and strings of onions. "Oh dear," he sighed. "One gold coin won't buy enough of these things to fill the palace."

He was just about to give up when he heard the sound of a shepherd boy playing a flute. An idea struck him at once.

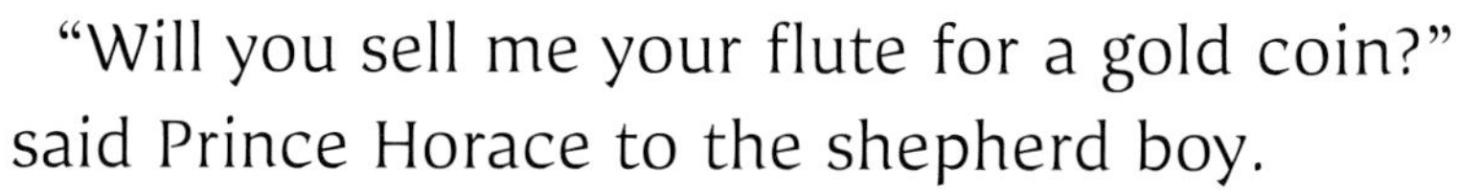

"Will you sell me your flute for a gold coin?" said Prince Horace to the shepherd boy.

"You bet!" came the reply. So the prince handed over the coin, and all the way home, he played a happy tune on his new flute.

Princess Emily spent all day searching the town for something to buy. "It's no good," she said. "The palace is just too big. I shall just have to tell Father that I have failed."

Then, as she turned the corner, her eye was caught by a glimmer of light from a small shop. She looked in at the window and saw the shopkeeper lighting candles and putting them in lanterns.

“Of course!” exclaimed the princess. She rushed into the shop and bought as many candles as she could. Then she ran back to the palace with her bundle, more pleased than a flea on a shaggy dog.

That evening, in the throne room, the king said to his three children, “Show me what you have bought, then I can choose who will succeed me.”

Prince Crispin brought in his feathers, which flew everywhere, and made everyone sneeze. When they had settled they only filled twenty rooms of the palace.

“Well done, a good try,” said the king.

“Oh flummocks!” said Prince Crispin.

Prince Horace took out the flute he’d bought. He put it to his lips and began to play a tune. When he had finished everyone looked very puzzled.

“Don’t you see,” said the prince, “I’ve filled the palace with music.”

"Brilliant!" said the king. "No one will beat that."

"Just a moment, Father," said Princess Emily. "Hadn't we better check that the music reached the cellar and the attic?"

"Quite right," said the king, sending two servants to the topmost and bottommost parts of the palace. "Now then, Horace, play again." His son played an even louder tune.

After a while the servants came back. "When are you going to start?" they said.

Prince Crispin grinned, "They haven't heard the music, so it hasn't filled the whole palace."

"Oh flummocks!" said Prince Horace.

So now it was the turn of Princess Emily. Everyone laughed when they saw her small bundle.

She opened it and sent the servants off to put candles into lanterns all over the palace.

"Make sure you put a lantern in every room," she ordered. "And don't forget the cellar and attic." Then she went around and lit every candle herself.

"There you are, Father," said the princess. "I've filled the whole palace ... with light."

The king was delighted and hugged his daughter. "You are the winner, three cheers for the future queen!"

"Oh double flummocks!" said her brothers.

Princess Emily became a good queen and her people were very happy. Every year after that, to celebrate her birthday, candles were lit in every house. This meant that, not just the palace, but the whole land was filled with light.

The wind and the sun

The wind had been cross all week. Huffing and puffing, he had blown down trees, stamped on fields of corn, and sent the chimney on top of Mrs. Crabtree's cottage crashing into her garden, just missing her cat.

He was in such a grumpy mood that he began to pick a quarrel with the sun. "I am much stronger than you," he boasted. "You can't blow down trees or nearly flatten a cat like I can. I could even blow clouds in front of you and blot out your sunshine. I am more powerful than anything else in the whole world."

The sun smiled at the wind and replied in a gentle voice, "I know you can do all that, but it doesn't mean that you are more powerful than I am."

"Of course it does, fire-face," roared the wind, blowing a sudden blast at some pigs which almost straightened their tails.

"Let's have a contest to see who's the strongest."

"All right," said the sun. "You see that man walking along the road. Well, I challenge you to see which of us can get his coat off."

"Ha!" puffed the wind with a gust of laughter. "I can do that before you can say 'Easy, peasy, brisk and breezy.'"

"We shall see," said the sun. "You can go first."

The wind took a deep, deep breath. Then he puffed out his cheeks and began to blow a terrific gale. He picked and plucked at the man's coat to try to get it off. It didn't work though, because the more the wind blew, the more the man tightened his belt and wrapped his coat around him.

The wind roared and whooshed with all his might; it was almost a hurricane. Once he even swept the man right off his feet.

The wind blew until he was blue in the face. Eventually he turned to the sun and whispered hoarsely, "I give up it's your turn now."

The sun gave a big, broad smile and shone down on the man as brightly as he could. Soon, the poor man had to stop and mop his forehead with a big spotted handkerchief.

"Any minute now," said the sun, sending down a burst of super-scorching sunshine. Sure enough, before the man had gone another thirty paces, he stopped and put down his suitcase again. Then he squinted up at the sun, puffed out his cheeks ... and took off his coat.

"Hooray!" cheered the sun, beaming. "Look at that, I've done it!"

The wind wheezed in his anger, for now he knew that he wasn't the most powerful in the world. Still out of breath, all he could manage to say was, "Oh blow!"

The three wishes

Max was a poor woodcutter who lived in a small cottage next to a large forest with his wife, Elsa.

One day, just as he was about to chop down a giant oak tree, he saw a woodland fairy fluttering just below a branch. He had never seen a fairy before. "Maybe I'm dreaming," he said to himself, rubbing his eyes; but when he opened them again, the fairy was still there.

"Hello!" said the tiny creature. "If you spare this oak tree, the next three wishes which you or your wife make will come true." Then she was gone. So Max left the oak tree and moved on to another.

He worked hard all day, and when he got home he was so tired that he had forgotten all about the fairy and the three wishes.

"I'm hungry, what's for supper?" he asked

"Potato soup," answered Elsa. "We haven't got enough money to buy meat."

"Not again," moaned Max. "I'll begin to look like a potato soon. I wish we could have a nice sausage for a change." No sooner had he spoken when there was a "Tring!", and a huge sausage appeared on the table.

This reminded Max of the fairy, and he immediately told Elsa about their three wishes. When he'd finished, Elsa was furious.

"You stupid man, you've wasted one of our precious wishes on a sausage! I wish it was stuck to the end of your nose."

Immediately there was another "Tring!", and the sausage flew from the table and attached itself to the end of Max's nose.

When he next spoke, it sounded as though he had a terrible cold. "Dow look what you've done," he mumbled. "Try and pull it off." Elsa tried, but the sausage was well and truly stuck on.

At last she said, "Let's ask for all the gold and jewels in the world. Then we could enjoy ourselves."

"Don't be silly. How could I enjoy byself wid everybody calling be sausage-dose?" replied Max. "Oh, I wish dis had dever happened."

"Tring!" The sausage disappeared, and so did their third and final wish. They sat down to their potato soup, and argued about whose fault it was.

If only they had eaten the sausage when it had first appeared, they would still have had two wishes left. If you had three wishes, what would you wish for?

The nightingale

In the days before cars, computers and corn flakes, there lived an emperor called Choo Ning. He was the Emperor of China – a very powerful man. The emperor's palace was the biggest and best in the world. It had the most beautiful gardens, which were so big that Choo Ning hadn't even seen most of them. They stretched for miles: over fields to a lake, and then on to a forest in which lived a nightingale. Beyond the forest was the sea. At night the fisherman would drift past, silently casting their nets and praying for a good catch. As they did so, they would hear the nightingale singing. To them it was a sign that their prayers had been heard.

Important people from many countries visited the emperor in his palace. When they returned home they would talk about their adventures, and always they remembered the nightingale and her beautiful song.

One day, a book arrived from the Queen of France. She had visited China the previous summer and had written about her travels. Choo Ning read the book with great pleasure, until he came to these words: "The Emperor of China has many amazing things, but the most amazing of all is the nightingale."

The emperor had never heard of a nightingale.

He summoned his chief adviser, and asked, "What's a nightingale? It's supposed to be the best thing I have, but I haven't a clue what it is. Find out or else I'll have you cleaning out the royal guinea pig cages for a year."

The chief adviser scuttled through the palace asking everyone what a nightingale was. No one knew.

Eventually he came to the kitchen, where a young maid was stirring the soup for supper that night.

"A nightingale?" she said. "It's a bird, of course. It sings every night in the forest."

"Go and get it straight away!" commanded the chief adviser.

"Only if you stir this soup," said the girl. "And say please." The chief adviser was so desperate that he did as she asked.

The girl ran to the forest, and soon found the tree in which the nightingale was already singing. "Excuse me, Nightingale, will you come to the palace and sing for the emperor, please?"

"All right," said the nightingale.

Later that evening, the emperor sat at his golden banqueting table facing a golden perch, on which the nightingale had been placed. The emperor nodded, and the nightingale began to sing. She sang many tunes; each was so beautiful, that the emperor had tears rolling down his cheeks, which made his beard all soggy.

"I shall keep you here in a cage," said the emperor when the bird had finished. "Then you can sing for me every day."

"But Emperor," replied the nightingale. "I sing songs of freedom."

"Don't worry, it will be a golden cage, the most valuable in China, if not the world."

Then the nightingale pleaded, "You can't tell the worth of something by what it looks like. What's inside is far more important. How can I build my nest if I am in a cage, even if it is made of gold?"

But the emperor's mind was made up, and the bird was put in the cage. Every evening she sang for Choo Ning.

Some weeks later a parcel arrived for the emperor. On it was a label: "To Choo Ning, I really enjoyed my visit. I loved hearing your nightingale, but how does this one compare with yours? Best wishes from the Emperor of Japan."

He opened the parcel and found a beautiful nightingale made of silver and gold, and studded with precious jewels. On the side was a key. It was a clockwork nightingale, and when it was wound up it sang a beautiful song.

"Bring me the real bird. We'll see which sings the best," said the emperor. The nightingale was brought and both birds sang. Then the emperor said, "Hmm, I suppose the old bird can sing more tunes, but it looks extremely shabby. Look how the new bird glitters and sparkles."

Now everyone wanted to marvel at the clockwork nightingale, and hear its one song. The chief adviser had to wind the bird fifty times. And fifty times the bird sang the same tune.

"Now let's hear the scruffy old nightingale again," said the emperor. But when they looked in the golden cage, it was empty. In the excitement, the door had come unfastened, and the nightingale had flown away. "Of all the cheek!" said the emperor. "That bird shall never be allowed in the palace again."

For a year the emperor listened to the clockwork nightingale as often as he could. Every visitor marvelled at the beauty of the jewelled bird and its wonderful song. But one day, while it was singing for the Queen of Siam, there was a "whirrrrr, clunk!" – and the bird stopped singing.

The royal clockmaker was called. She examined the inside of the bird, then shook her head and said, "Your Excellency, these clockwork parts are very worn. I've done what I can, but the bird should only be made to sing once a day."

Choo Ning became very sad. The only time he ever smiled was when the clockwork nightingale sang its one and only song each day, and even then he wished it could sing other tunes as well.

Several years passed and the emperor lay ill in bed close to death. He opened his eyes from time to time to look at the silver and gold bird. "Please sing for me," he pleaded. But the bird had long since broken. It just looked at him dumbly. Then, through the window he heard a song: a strange, yet familiar song. He turned his head and saw the real nightingale land on his windowsill.

The bird had answered the emperor's plea, and once more sang tunes that he had not heard for many years. Eventually Choo Ning sighed deeply and closed his eyes.

When he awoke the nightingale was still there.

"You have saved my life," he said. "Will you always come if I promise to let you return to your forest?"

"Yes I will," replied the nightingale. "But only if you promise to tell no one about me. This way I will be left in peace."

The emperor nodded. "Very well," he said.

"Then I will come," continued the bird. "And I will sing about places and things you cannot see from your palace. My songs will make you a great ruler. I have already shown you one of the most important things you can know: that you cannot tell a person's worth by what's on the outside."

Choo Ning looked back at his old clockwork nightingale, and as he did so one of its wings fell off and fell to the floor with a jangling crash. He smiled, and nodded again.

So the emperor got out of bed, much to everyone's surprise. He lived many more years, and with the help of the nightingale became one of the wisest and kindest emperors China ever had.

Clever Millie

On top of a small, high hill lived a woman named Millie Smith and her husband. He was an enormous man, with muscles as strong as iron. No one knew his first name. He was just known as Big Smithy.

There were two problems with the Smiths' house. Firstly it faced north, so there was always a cold wind whistling in through the doors and windows, even in the summer. Secondly, their well was at the bottom of the hill, and it was such a struggle for Millie to carry the full bucket back up again.

Big Smithy was a lazy man. He made his wife do all the work while he boasted about his strength. "I'm the strongest person in the whole land," he'd say. Then to prove it he'd throw a rock six fields across the valley. "My strength can beat anything."

"Brains are better," said Millie, the cleverer of the two.

"Well you can't be very clever to think that," said Big Smithy, and laughed at the thought that he had outwitted his wife. But the next week, Millie Smith got the chance to prove her point.

It was Friday lunchtime when Millie arrived home from town with the week's shopping.

"Are you sure you're the strongest in the land?" she asked Big Smithy, who was busy reading the paper.

"Of course I am," he boomed. "Why?"

"Well, there was a man in town who said that *he* was," came the reply.

Big Smithy stopped reading, and suddenly looked very worried. "Was he over seven feet tall with red hair, a red beard, staring eyes and fists the size of water melons?" he said.

His wife thought for a bit. "Yes, that's him. He called himself ... er, now what was it?"

"Boris," said Big Smithy quietly, his eyes wide and staring.

"Yes, that's it. Do you know him?"

"Know him?" yelled Big Smithy. "I'm afraid I've been lying to you all this time. I'm not the strongest in the land, he is. Only he's been in the south for years, I never thought he'd come up this way." He stopped and thought for a minute. "Maybe he's just up for the day. Yes, that's it, he'll be on his way home by now."

"Fraid not," said Millie, looking out of the window. "He's coming across the valley towards the house, look!"

Big Smithy screamed, jumped up and ran around the room wildly. "He'll pummel me, he'll bash me, he'll ... mangle-ize me! What am I going to do?"

"Well ..." said his wife.

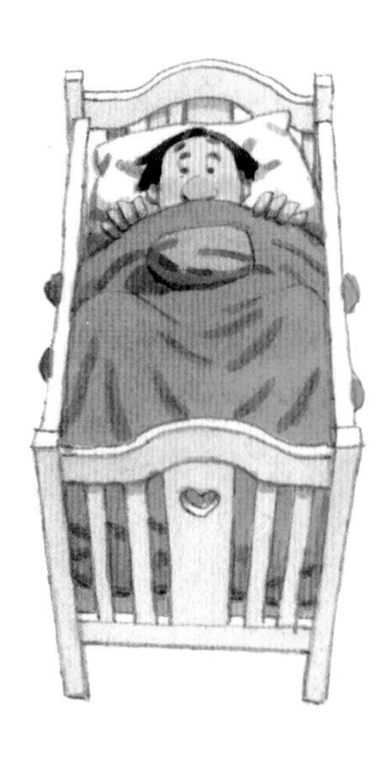

"Millie, you haven't got an idea, have you?"

"What'll you do if I help you?" she said.

"Anything, I'll do anything," he replied, going whiter than a polar bear in a snowstorm.

"Right," she said, squeezing him into a small cot in the corner. "Now stay there, don't say a word and hold this," and she handed him a big rock.

Ten long minutes passed. Then they heard a knock at the door, so loud that it rattled all the windows. Millie Smith opened it and there stood the enormous figure of Boris. He was even bigger than she remembered.

"Where's Big Smithy?" he said, spitting out the words like grape seeds.

"He's not in," said Millie. "He's away in the south. He said he was going down there to find a man named Boris. Then he said he was going to bash him to bits and squash him to a jelly."

"What!" said the man. "I am Boris!"

"Oh, that's funny," said Millie, looking him up and down. "He said you were big and strong."

Boris snorted with anger. "I am big and strong. I am bigger and stronger than he is."

"Then you'll be able to do anything he can do."

"And more," said Boris. "I am Boris the Brave! I am Boris the Brilliant! I am Boris the, er ..." but he couldn't think of anything else beginning with B.

Millie wondered why so many men spent so much time boasting about how great they were. Then she said, "Every day, Big Smithy turns the house around to the south so it gets the sun."

"That's a child's job," said Boris, taking off his jacket, which could have doubled as a tent. He put his shoulder against the house, and heaved and huffed. With a huge scraping and rumbling, the house was slowly turned all the way around. Millie blinked into the sunshine, and breathed in the nice warm breeze.

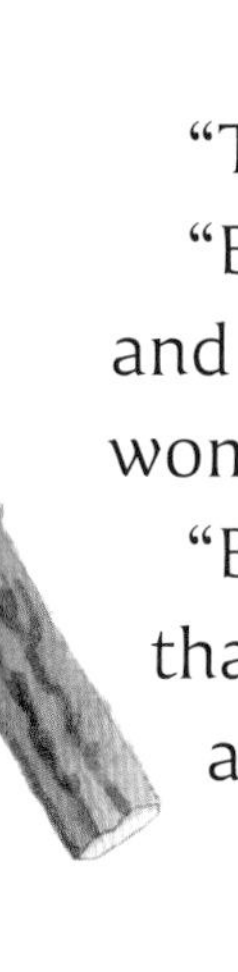

"There," said Boris. "What else can he do?"

"Big Smithy's so strong, he could take a long stick and drive it right through the hill," said the clever woman.

"Baby's job!" said Boris, and he went to get a log that was as tall as the house. Then he raised the log above his head, and with a huge shout he drove it downwards so hard that it disappeared completely into the hill.

"There!" he said triumphantly. Millie looked into the hole, and dropped a small pebble in. There was a moment's silence, then ... "splash." The pebble had hit some water. She had a well at the top of the hill.

"Now you'd better go down south and fight Big Smithy," said Millie.

Boris was quite tired, although he didn't say so. "I think I'll have some bread first," he said, and pushed his way into the house. It was then that he saw Big Smithy in the cot.

"Big Smithy!" he snarled, and strode across the room towards him. Smithy was so scared that he started to shake. He clenched his fist so hard around the rock Millie had given him, that it shattered into a million pieces.

Just before Boris reached the cot, Millie shouted, "Watch out Boris, that's Baby Smithy. If you harm him, Big Smithy won't be very pleased."

Boris stopped. "*Baby Smithy?*" he said, looking at the size of the person in the cot. Then he glanced at the crushed rock on the floor and suddenly felt very weak. He rushed out of the door, down the hill and was never seen around those parts again.

Big Smithy was so scared that he shook for three days afterwards. He was true to his word, though, and eventually he said, "You were right Millie Smith: brains are best. I suppose you'll want me to do all the jobs around the house now."

"No," said Millie. "Just do half of them ... and stop boasting." And so the two of them lived happily for the rest of their days.

The lonely giant

Bigg, the giant, was always playing tricks on people. Sometimes he would stomp on the ground to make an earthquake. At other times he would cough to make a sound like thunder. His best trick, though, was to disguise his nose as a hill. Then as people climbed up to the top, he'd sneeze and tumble them all down again. He always laughed when his tricks worked, but deep down Bigg was very unhappy; he was a lonely giant.

One day, he saw an old woman walking through the forest. He decided to do his thunder-cough so she would think it was about to rain; but rather than run home to take in her washing, she turned on him.

"So, you thought you could give me a fright, eh? Well, I don't want one, thank you." Bigg was taken aback, after all, she was so small and he was so ... well, big. "I can give you something that *you* want though," she said. "Happiness. I bet I can make you happy within a day."

"What do you bet?" asked Bigg, who was becoming very interested.

"If I make you happy, you must promise never to play another trick on anyone," answered the old woman.

"What if you don't make me happy?" he said.

"Then I will be your servant forever."

Bigg could never resist a challenge, especially one he was sure to win. Because even if by some chance she did make him happy, he wouldn't admit it. So he said, "All right!"

"Good, let's have a drink to settle it," said the old woman, handing Bigg a bottle.

"What have I got to lose?" said Bigg, gulping down the liquid in one swallow. However, no sooner had he finished, when there was a large flash. Bigg started to feel his head spin. Then he started to shrink. He got smaller and smaller until he was staring up at the old woman. In fact he was child-sized.

"You tricked me!" he said.

"Don't worry. The magic only lasts for a day," replied the woman. "After that you will turn back into a giant again." Then she turned and walked away.

Bigg walked into the town. When he was a giant it only used to take him ten strides, but now it took ten minutes. With each step he got more and more sulky and miserable.

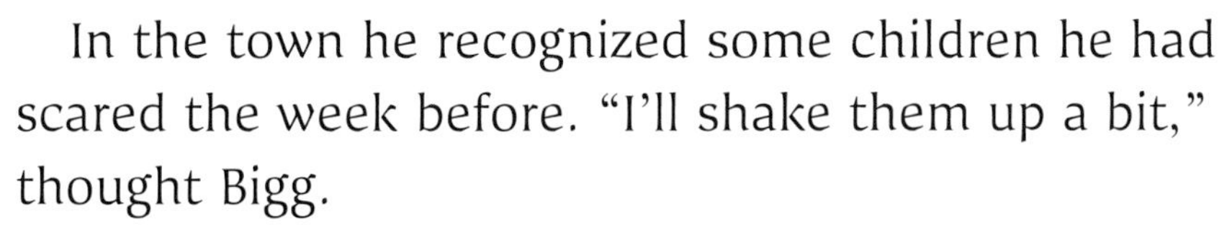

In the town he recognized some children he had scared the week before. "I'll shake them up a bit," thought Bigg.

Forgetting he was now the same size as them, he stomped on the ground to make them think it was an earthquake. But as he was small, nothing happened and the children just looked at him in amazement.

"Look at that boy, he's doing a dance," said one.

They all loved dancing, so they immediately joined in, jumping and stomping next to Bigg.

Next, Bigg thought he'd frighten them – so he opened his mouth wide and roared with all his might.

"Look, he's being a lion," the children said. "Let's do it too!" And they did.

Finally Bigg shouted, "Listen – I'm a giant!"

The children laughed wildly. "First he dances, then he pretends to be a lion, now he tells jokes!"

Bigg had never felt so angry and embarrassed. He stomped off, but they came after him.

"Don't go! Stay and play with us. You're fun."

Bigg decided that he would. He thought, "After all, I might find out some new ways to frighten them when I'm a giant again."

They played lots of games all afternoon, then Bigg went home with one of them for dinner. When the family found out that he had nowhere to sleep, they let him have their spare bedroom. It had the most comfortable bed Bigg had ever slept in.

The next morning, he taught the children some games that he used to play when he was a young giant. He was having a lovely day, the sort you hope will never end.

In the afternoon, however, during a game of hide-and-seek in the forest, Bigg came across the old woman, and remembered it was time to turn back into a giant.

Before the old woman could say anything, Bigg cried, "You win, I am happy! *Very* happy. Please don't make me change back into a giant." Then he fell to his knees, sobbing loudly.

Smiling, the old woman reached into her pocket. "This will keep you small," she said giving him another bottle. "Now I must get my washing in, it looks like there may be a thunderstorm."

"Thank you!" Bigg shouted after her, and took the stopper out of the bottle.

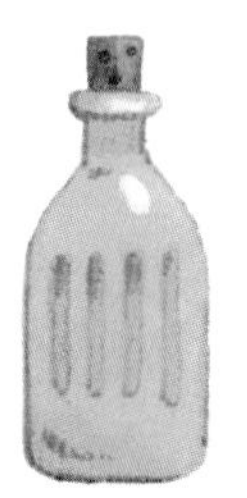

The other children arrived just as Bigg was finishing the drink. Then together they went into the town for dinner, Bigg grinning from ear to ear.

"By the way, we haven't asked you what your name is," said one of the children.

Bigg thought for a minute. "It's Tiny," he said.

The golden windows

Mary was a young girl who lived with her mother in a house on the side of a valley. From her garden she could look across the valley to another house. It was a very special one because it had golden windows.

Mary had always longed to visit this house. As she played in the garden she would often stop and gaze at the beautiful windows shimmering like flames in the afternoon sun. Then she would sigh and say to herself, "I wish I could live in a house like that. It must be wonderful to look out through golden windows."

Sometimes she would ask her mother to take her across the valley for a walk. But her mother would say, "Not today, Mary, I've got so much to do. Maybe another day, when I'm not so busy."

For her seventh birthday, Mary's grandmother gave her a shiny new bicycle. Mary was thrilled, and it wasn't long before she was an expert rider. As there wasn't much traffic along the lane next to her house, Mary was allowed to go for short rides on her own. Then one day, she had an idea.

"Mother," she asked. "Please may I ride across the valley? I'd really love to go and see the house with the golden windows."

Mary's mother knew that Mary rode her bike very sensibly, so she said, "All right, but do be careful, and ..."

"Thanks!" said Mary, rushing out of the house.

"And be back in time for dinner!" shouted her mother after her.

Mary set off, keeping very close to the side of the road, and going around each bend with great care. As she got closer to the house, she became more and more excited. At last she would be able to see the golden windows close up. Maybe, if she was really lucky, the people who lived in the house would let her touch them.

Eventually she reached the front gate of the house. She propped her bicycle against the hedge and lifted the latch. "I'll wait until I'm in the garden before I look," she thought, holding her breath with anticipation. "I can hardly wait."

However, as she opened the gate, she could contain herself no longer. She must look at those beautiful golden windows. But as she raised her head, her heart sank; her tingle of excitement had just turned into an ache of disappointment.

"But they're glass, just plain old glass," she said softly, closely to tears. "They're ... they're just ... ordinary. And all the time I thought they were made of gold."

She didn't bother to go any further. She closed the gate, picked up her bicycle, and turned it around ready for the long ride home. As she set off, she glanced across the valley and saw something which made her stop. She could see her own house – and the windows were gold! They were blazing like golden flames. Then she realized why: they too were reflecting the rays of the afternoon sun. So she did live in a house with golden windows after all.

The miller, his son and their donkey

One day, a miller and his son were taking their donkey to sell at a market in a nearby town. On the way they met a group of young girls.
"Look!" said one of them, pointing. "Imagine trudging along this dusty road when one of them could be riding on the donkey. How silly!"

The miller was a kind man, so he said to his son, "That's a good idea. You have a ride. Up you get." And he helped his son on to the donkey.

They carried on with their journey and, after a while, they came across two old men. "Hey, miller!" shouted one. "That son of yours is a real lazy-bones. He's the one who should be walking, not you."

"Hmm, perhaps they are right," said the miller, and changed places with his son.

They rode on a little further, and then they met a small crowd of women and children. One of the women pointed at them and said, "You selfish old man! Why don't you let the poor boy ride, too?"

"She's got a point, there," said the miller, and he lifted up his son behind him. They carried on with their journey, both riding the donkey.

They had almost reached the town, when a man coming the other way asked, "Is that your donkey?"

"Yes it is," answered the miller. "We're taking him to sell at the market. Why do you ask?"

"Well, the poor old beast will soon be worn out, carrying you two," said the man, stroking the donkey's nose. "Who'll want to buy him then? Surely it would be much better if you carried the donkey."

The miller and his son looked at each other.

"That's a very good idea," said the miller, and with the help of a strong pole and some rope, they carried the donkey into town.

The people of the town had never seen anything so funny before.

"Just look at that!" said one man. "They're trying to carry a donkey." They all laughed until tears rolled down their cheeks.

Now, the donkey didn't mind being carried, but he hated being laughed at. So he kicked and struggled at the rope until it broke with a "Snap!" Then he galloped out of the town and was never seen again.

The miller and his son walked sadly home. "I shouldn't have tried to please so many people," he said with a sigh. "I ended up pleasing no one. It looks like I'm the donkey now."

Princess Tabatha's new trick

King Theodore and Queen Phoebe were much loved by everyone in the land. However, the same could not be said about their daughter, Princess Tabatha. She was what might be called a royal little beast.

Tabatha loved to play tricks on people. Her best ones were: putting peanut butter on the underside of the door handles so that the servants kept getting their hands messy, and creeping up on the cook's cat when it was asleep, then barking loudly like a dog which made it yowl with fright. The trick she loved best, though, was to raise the drawbridge just as the royal limousine was arriving at the palace. She loved to see it screech to a halt in front of the moat.

She would have put big spiders in the beds of important visitors, but for the fact she was scared stiff of spiders.

One day, Princess Tabatha was in her private bathroom. The queen thought she was brushing her teeth, but really she was making water bombs to drop from the window on to the castle guards. She filled the last bag with water, then went to unlock the door. The key was stuck. She tugged harder, and eventually it turned, but Tabatha had had an idea. The water bombs were forgotten in a splash.

Tabatha locked the door again, then started to cry loudly, "Help, I'm stuck in the bathroom! He-e-e-elp!" The cook heard the loud screams, left her baking and rushed up the stairs. She tried hard to open the door, while inside Princess Tabatha just sat on the edge of the bathtub and read a comic.

After ten minutes, Tabatha turned the key, opened the door and said with a mischievous smile, "Oh dear, silly me forgot to unlock it."

The cook was about to tell her off, when the smoke alarm went off in the kitchen. "My cakes!" she cried, and rushed downstairs.

On Saturday, when she knew a servant was in the middle of loading the washing machine, Princess Tabatha tried the same trick. "Help, I'm stuck in the bathroom! He-e-e-lp!" It worked again. As the servant rushed up the stairs, she opened the door and said, "That made you run!"

He was so cross that he put too much detergent in the washing machine, which made it overflow with bubbles.

That evening the king and queen had to go to a very important state banquet. Shirley, the babysitter, was watching a detective series on the television when she heard, "Help, I'm stuck in the bathroom! He-e-e-elp!"

"Coming!" shouted Shirley. Then she jumped up and ran upstairs as fast as she could.

She was met by a smiling Princess Tabatha who said, "That had you worried!"

Shirley said crossly, “One day you’ll try that trick and no one will believe you!” This woke the young princes, who started screaming, so Shirley had to quieten them down. By the time she went back to the television, she’d missed the end of the show.

Over the next few days the naughty princess tried her trick on just about everyone. Then on Wednesday evening her parents were enjoying an evening off, when there came a huge scream.

“Mother! Father! I’m stuck in the bathroom with a massive spider! He-e-elp!” The king and queen knew how scared she was of spiders. They rushed to the bathroom, but try as they might, they could not open the door. Inside, Tabatha continued to cry.

“She must be telling the truth,” said the queen.

“I’m calling the fire department,” said the king. Soon, a wailing siren could be heard in the castle courtyard. The firemen rushed in and started attacking the door with their axes. They broke it down, only to find Tabatha sitting in the bathtub reading a book.

"Where's the fire?" she said, with a grin. The king went as red as a fire engine, and apologized profusely.

One night during the following week, after the shattered bathroom door had been repaired, Princess Tabatha went to her bathroom to get a drink of water. The door, being new, was a bit stiff, and as she went to leave, she found it stuck. She tugged and pulled as hard as she could for ages, but with no success. The door was stuck fast, really stuck.

She sat down on the edge of the bathtub. She'd just started to think how she could turn this into her best trick yet, when her eyes rested on something which made her blood run cold. Crawling out of the drain in the bathtub was the biggest, blackest, hairiest spider she'd ever seen.

She leapt across the room and pressed herself against the wall, staring at the spider, who was now on the edge of the bathtub. It really was a monster.

For a full minute she was too terrified to shout, but when she did it was very loud. "AAGHH! SPIDER! HELP! I'M STUCK! AAAGGHH!"

Soon she heard the king's voice outside the door.

"Sorry Tabatha, you've tried that trick once too often – we're not falling for it again. You can come out whenever you want to. Goodnight." And he went back to bed.

Tabatha spent the worst night of her life. Although the spider went to sleep on the edge of the bathtub, Tabatha thought it was wide awake and ready to pounce. So she stood, rigid, glued to the wall, her eyes fixed on the spider all night.

In the morning, the spider had just disappeared down the drain when her father pushed open the door to discover his white-faced daughter.

"No harm done," he said, looking into the empty bathtub. "You'd better get to bed now."

Princess Tabatha was too tired to protest. She got into bed, and soon went to sleep; but she woke up a completely different girl.

Silly McAdam

Not too long ago there lived a man called Adam McAdam. His wife called him something different. She worked very hard, but Adam McAdam always seemed to lose their money; so she called him Silly McAdam.

"You drive me around the bend!" she'd often scream, which is what some people would say when they are at their wits' end.

Now you might think Mrs. McAdam was a bit of a nag; but she wasn't. She was just an extremely nice woman married to an extremely silly man.

One morning, after a week in which Adam McAdam had been especially silly, his wife was counting their money. It didn't take long.

"Two buttons and an old bus ticket. We're broke thanks to you," she said. "You drive me around the bend!"

"Sorry," he replied.

"We don't even have enough to buy a piece of pizza. There's nothing left to do, you'll have to go to an old junk sale. There's one in town this afternoon. Come on, we'll look for some old stuff – we must have something that people will want to buy."

They both hunted in the attic, searched in the cellar, and grubbed around in the garage. At the end of the morning, they looked at the pile of assorted junk. There was a tennis racket with three strings, a jigsaw puzzle with some pieces missing, a lamp in the shape of a ship, an old wooden toilet seat and lots more not-very-useful things.

"This lot should be worth something," said Mrs. McAdam. "Though it's a pity we don't have one decent thing to sell."

After they had loaded up the car, Adam McAdam got the old leather flying helmet and goggles that he always wore for driving. (As he drove along, he liked to pretend he was flying a plane, and he used the horn to shoot down enemy planes.)

"Of course! Why didn't I think of it before?" said Mrs. McAdam. "You can sell that silly old helmet. It's pretty old, so it's sure to be worth quite a bit."

"Oh, but I love that helmet ... " complained Adam; but he stopped when he saw the look on his wife's face. "I'll sell it," he sighed.

Adam McAdam drove his car down the road towards the town. As he bumped along (the car was very old) he saw his friend Wally walking along in the same direction. He slowed down and stopped next to him.

"Hello Wally, do you want a lift?"

"No thanks," said Wally, "I'm just looking for somewhere to sit to eat my lunch." At the mention of the word "lunch," Adam McAdam's tummy gave a loud grumble.

"I'll trade you something for your lunch," he said, jumping out and opening the car. There was nothing that Wally wanted, until his noticed the old leather flying helmet on Adam's head.

In a minute, Adam was driving along chewing a peanut butter sandwich, without his flying helmet, which was now Wally's. When he reached the town, he suddenly realized he had no idea where the junk sale was to be held, so he stopped to ask a man. As he pulled over, his wheels hit a pothole, and the back door flew open.

The man stopped and looked inside the car.

"I expect you're going to the junk sale," he said.

"Yes, how did you know?" said Adam.

"Oh just a hunch," replied the man. "Tell you what, I'll give you ten gold coins for all of it." He had worked out that if he sold Adam's junk, he'd get much more.

"Ten gold coins?" said Adam.

"All right, eleven, I can't say fairer than that. But you'll have to throw the car in as well."

"Ok," said Adam, handing the man the car keys. Adam McAdam was just about to head home when a noise stopped him in his tracks. He looked up the road and saw a woman with a one-man band. She was playing to a large crowd who clapped loudly and threw money into her hat.

"That's a good way of making money," thought Adam McAdam. He went up to the woman.

"I'll give you eleven gold coins for your band," he said.

"OK," she replied. "I'm far too old for this anyway." Adam McAdam began to play the one-man band. Very soon he realized there was a problem with his plan: he had never played music before. The noise he made was worse than terrible.

The crowd started to boo him, and shout rude things such as, "Shut up!" and "I can't bear it!" One woman said, "Sounds like six cats fighting in a dustbin!" Then one by one they all went away covering their ears, leaving Adam McAdam alone. There was nothing to do but head for home.

It took him ages, as the one-man band was very heavy. He had nearly arrived at his house, when he saw Wally again.

Wally said, "Please help me, Adam. It's my son's birthday tomorrow and I haven't got him a present yet, and now all the shops are closed."

Adam thought, then had a brain wave. "What about this!" he said, pointing to the one-man band.

"Brilliant!" shouted Wally. "Oh, but I don't have any money."

"I'll trade it for my old leather flying helmet," said Adam. And the two men swapped again.

So it was that Adam McAdam arrived home.

"Did you sell the stuff?" asked his wife.

"Er ... yes," he replied.

"Well at least you've done something right. Give me the money, please."

"I traded it for a one-man band," said Adam.

"Well give me that, then," said his wife.

"I traded it with Wally for my old flying helmet," he replied.

"Why did he have your helmet, you silly man?" asked his wife.

"Because I traded it for his lunch on my way to town," he said again.

Mrs McAdam's eyes grew wide, and she started to shake with rage. "You drive me around the bend!" she said through clenched teeth. "You mean to tell me you left with a load of stuff and a flying helmet, and you've come back with just the helmet?"

"Well ... um ... yes," said Silly Adam.

"Silly McAdam!" she shouted. "You've driven me around the bend long enough – now I'm going to drive *you* around the bend!"

"But you can't. I sold the car as well."

"Then I'll use this!" she said, picking up a walking stick. She chased him out of the house, and true to her word she drove him right around the bend.

The giving tree

Once there was a forest where few people ever went. In the middle of this forest was a clearing in which stood a tree, its trunk was straight and tall, its branches were strong, its leaves were beautiful and its fruit tasted like heaven.

One morning the tree awoke, as usual, to the chorus of birds and other forest creatures. It stretched its branches and rustled its leaves to greet the new day. Then it looked down and saw a basket, in which slept a small baby girl.

The tree waited, but no one came for it. After a while the baby woke up and started to cry.

"You're hungry," said the tree. "You can have my fruit." The tree shook one of its branches. A fruit fell into the baby's mouth and turned immediately into juice sweeter than mother's milk.

Six times during that day the baby cried, and each time the tree fed her with its fruit. The next morning, the basket and the baby had gone.

Ten years later, a young girl stood in front of the tree. "Don't you recognize me?" she said. "I was the baby you fed. What will you give me now?"

"You can have my twigs and leaves," said the tree. The girl climbed the tree and played in its branches. She swung on them, used them as a tightrope, then broke off a large twig and made it into a sword for a game of pirates. In the heat of the day, the tree's leaves shaded the girl from the sun. As evening came, the girl left.

Some years later the girl came back. Now she was a teenager. "What will you give me?" she asked.

"You can have my branches," said the tree. So the girl sawed the branches off the tree, and took them away to build herself a wooden house.

More years passed. When the girl came back, she was a young woman. "What will you give me now?"

"You can have my trunk," said the tree.

The girl chopped down the trunk, and from it made a dug-out canoe. Then she took it to the sea and set off on her travels. The tree was now a stump.

Many years passed. Then one day an old woman stood next to the tree stump.

The woman asked, "What will you give me now?"

The tree replied, "I have no more to offer you than what I am. You can have my stump."

The old woman sat down. "All these years you have given me food, shelter, play and travel. Now what can I give you, Tree?"

"I was there at your beginning, and now I am the last page in your book. Tell me about your life."

So the old woman told the tree all about her life and travels: the people and places she had seen and been to. The tree listened. As night drew on, the old woman didn't leave. She curled up on the stump and fell asleep for the last time.

That night something magical happened, and next morning, in that clearing in the forest where few people ever went, there stood the tree. It was more beautiful, and wiser, than it had ever been.

With thanks to Ray Gibson, Ronald Lloyd
Christopher Rawson, Kate Davies and Rachel Firth

Additional design by Reuben Barrance, Nayera Everall and Candice Whatmore
Digital manipulation by Will Dawes

This edition first published in 2007 by Usborne Publishing Ltd,
Usborne House, 83-85 Saffron Hill, London EC1N 8RT
www.usborne.com

Printed in Dubai.